Neil Bartlett was born in Chichester in 1958. He is the artistic director of the Lyric Theatre, London. His works for the theatre include *A Vision of Love Revealed in Sleep* and the music-theatre piece *Sarrasine*; translations include Racine's *Berenice*, Molière's *The Misanthrope* and Genet's *Splendide's*. Neil Bartlett is the author of *Who Was That Man?*, a biography of Oscar Wilde, and *Ready to Catch Him Should He Fall*, his first novel – both published by Serpent's Tail.

D0772032

Praise for *Mr Clive & Mr Page*

'This is a book remarkable for the way in which it teases and tantalises the reader into now pressing on to discover what will happen next and now turning back to discover what precisely has happened already . . . A writer who can really change the way people feel' Francis King

'Neil Bartlett's second novel establishes him among English fiction's fiercest historians of gay male suffering. His first novel, *Ready to Catch Him Should He Fall* (1991), was memorable, not least for its awesome record of the horrors of queer-bashing. *Mr Clive & Mr Page* is another sad story, this time about covert gay passions in London in the 1920s and 50s.' *TLS*

'Neil Bartlett is a man of many talents: actor, playwright, translator and now Artistic Director of the Lyric Theatre, Hammersmith, London. It is perhaps not surprising then, that we have had to wait for the appearance of his second novel, *Mr Clive & Mr Page*. And it has proved well worth the wait. Here we have a mesmeric, haunting novel which generates enormous atmosphere.' *Gay Times*

'This novel gives many pleasures: most striking, though is its portrayal of the bitter, narrow-minded spread of English manners and social norms as experienced by gay men of all classes. *Mr Clive & Mr Page* is less an amatory exercise of the past; more a timely dissection, both cool and chilling of the legacy of "Englishness". It is a fine, mature book and probably Bartlett's best.' *New Statesman*

Mr Clive & Mr Page

Neil Bartlett

Library of Congress Catalog Card Number: 95–72968

A complete catalogue record for this book can be obtained from
the British Library on request

The right of Neil Bartlett to be identified as the author of this
work has been asserted by him in accordance with the Copyright,
Designs and Patents Act 1988

First published in 1996 by
Serpent's Tail, 4 Blackstock Mews, London N4

First published in this edition 1998

Set in 10pt Plantin and 11pt Bodoni by Intype London Ltd
Printed in Great Britain by Mackays of Chatham, plc

10 9 8 7 6 5 4 3 2 1

Šis romāns ir veltīts maniem kolēģiem Rīgā,
Čikāgā un Londonā, un Dzintaram Rubesam.

It's a sordid business, isn't it, a suicide?
I suppose we shall have to give evidence?

Terence Rattigan, *The Deep Blue Sea*, 1952

Men are ever seeking their comforts and to achieve their ideals. Ours is a home-making, home-loving race. I think that the desire is in all of us to receive the family home from the past generation and to hand it on to the next with some good work of our own visible upon it. Rarely can this be accomplished in times of rapid change. Families cannot hold and have not held even to the same localities much less homes generation after generation, but we can at least preserve some memory of the old. In times such as these the maintenance and due consideration of the hopes and works of the generations that came before us seems a duty all the more sacred.

My father's house was very attractive to me. I well remember when he built it, and though I was then as small a boy as you are now the odor of fresh plastering remains in my nostrils even in this long retrospect. I can still see, also, the pane of golden glass let into the hallway door, which glowed so strangely, and which to my childish eye seemed to give an effect like that of sunlight even on the cloudy and snow-bound afternoons of the Chicago winters that I spent there. Much of what I describe here will I hope be well known to you already by the time that you come to read this, since these rooms will, I trust, have been witness to much of your growing up. Many of their features will perhaps be dear to you in memory. My purpose here is to give you some account of how they came to be built.

I am conscious as I write that the span of years between us is made to seem even greater than that usual between Grandfather and Grandson by the accident of my life having been spent and my fortune having been largely made in the century past, whereas yours will be lived and made in that yet mostly to come. Your times will be the ones of which generations past have only dreamt.

When you are of an age when you may care to review your memories of this house all that we thought modern may well seem the relics of a vanished time. All the more reason then why you should understand by whom and according to what principles it was conceived and constructed. My account may also serve to give to others not in any way related some indication of how a man of moderate fortune might live in the later part of that nineteenth century and hope to see life lived in the earlier part of this, the twentieth – an average man, with a modicum of this world's material possessions, but by no means rich, except in his friends, in his family and most especially in his marriage.

This house was begun in 1886. On the morning of June the first of that year I sat down in my London office to write to your Grandmother, as I did every day during that period between my departure for this country and her arrival in it, and told her of the scenes of demolition and digging on this corner of Brooke Street and Gilbert Street. How long ago and chaotic that day now seems as I sit here and write amidst the well-appointed calm of the room occupying that very corner! Just eighteen months after that day, such was the industry of the builders, we stood on the threshold of the house together, your Mother with us, she being at that time barely seven years of age. Such was the expert plan of the house, we had been able to move all our possessions under the carriage arch on Gilbert Street and to place them in our new home almost without witness. The first that our new neighbours knew of our arrival was the sight of us standing proudly and as a family in front of Mr Richardson's noble façade for all to see.

Here in her new home your Grandmother at once set about running the house in that spirit of open cheer that had lent such life and charm to the old Chicago house on the north-east corner of State and Goethe. Amongst our new friends in those first years were some of the leading London artists and writers of the time, as well as leading figures from the world of commerce. Those dinners, so expertly furnished, and with the guests so carefully selected, performed the office of that ancient task, the kindling of the hearth. They quickly won us a secure place in the Society of this city. A story apropos: our acquaintance and close neighbour Mrs James said to me, in all seriousness, "Mr Vail, you are a very important member of Society: you have a position of great prominence and influence. You get the latter from your wife and the former from your remarkable house." Do not think I thought this a disparagement, for I would have everyone know that I selected the one and built the other.

Those first years were a time when many of the great men engaged in building up the commerce of Chicago were visiting the capitals of Europe, seeking all that was best both in thought and in manufacture, amongst them my own contemporaries in the world of retailing, the young H.G. Selfridge, Mr Frank W. Woolworth and, of course, Marshall Field himself. My friendship with Mr Field was to be cemented when he was our guest here during his London visit of 1888. It was the then new interiors of this house that were partly responsible for his decision to later feature the work of Morris and Co. so vigorously in his World's Fair promotion. Gordon Selfridge has become a frequent Sunday visitor since. Our shared determination to bring to the Old World the innovations of the New has made us close colleagues; the work of Vail, Cottingham and Company, Engineers is, I am proud to say, an important and much-valued feature of his new premises on Oxford Street.

This house was designed by Henry Hobson Richardson of Brookline, Mass. He was the contemporary of Burnham and Root; I was acquainted with his work in our native city and considered it to be amongst the best and most progressive in the architectural arts of our time. He was in that period engaged in supervising the construction of the new store on State Street for Marshall Field; although involved in the equipping of those premises, I had not met him. Your Grandmother and I were to make his acquaintance through a mutual friend, the artist Hubert Herkomer, at a dinner given in the autumn of 1885 at the newly completed Prairie Street home of the Glessner family. We were both equally struck by the expression of a certain noble domestic ideal in the construction of the Glessner house, and at once conceived the notion of such a house becoming our future home. Little did we think it was to be in another country entirely. It was with some trepidation that I made the approach, knowing Mr Richardson to be advanced in years and unlikely to travel; on receiving his reply to our initial query I was heartened to know that here was a man in deepest sympathy with our own belief that a house should reflect the life lived within it. Thus began our collaboration.

From what he told me I am convinced that this house of ours is the one of all that he built that Richardson would most like to have lived in. It was his last work, and he would often refer to it in his letters to me, and I think he did this only half in jest, as "The House Beautiful". This term was one that we had used in our first letter to him. We had ourselves first heard it from the mouth of Mr Oscar Wilde during his lecture given on that subject in February 1882 at the Central Music Hall in Chicago – a man since much reviled but of whom it is still customary to speak with some respect in this house, even though this custom has been the subject of some comment amongst our London neighbours. Mr Richardson had I think as much an idea of the House Technical as of the House Beautiful; however, beautiful it indeed is. It is his monument. Just three weeks before his death Mr Richardson wrote me a note accompanying the finished drawings for the Brooke Street elevation, "There, Mr Vail, if I were to live five years longer, that is the last thing I would do on your house; my part is finished." It is his portrait, by Herkomer, that now hangs amongst the family pictures in the library.

Simplicity and proportion were the strongest characteristics of his work; those unseen parts were designed and finished with as much care and honesty as the more public rooms. The same style and finish go all through this house from the front to the back. No single detail was left unconsidered.

The roof is of red baked tiles, unglazed, and the outside walls are red also, being of a sombre yet rich-toned granite, hammered – a stone that looks well both in the sunlight of a London spring and when patterned by the snow of a Chicago winter. The idea I think was in Mr Richardson's mind that our house here should look well in, and withstand, storms far more severe than any which the environs of Oxford Street might ever be expected to weather! The interior walls, panelled and painted to Mr Richardson's own specifications, are all as hardwearing of finish as they are rich in colouring; the bathroom and kitchen fittings throughout are silver-plated rather than nickel, in the interests of hygiene and durability as well as of luxury. Even the window fittings were carefully chosen so that the whole house could be secure against draughts and exposure. The servicing of the house was a feature of the design to which particular thought was given, and the hidden Gilbert Street corridors, linked to each other and to the staff quarters at their northern end by a single staircase, all walled and floored alike in the finest white Minton tiling, give remarkably sudden and convenient access to all those areas of the house in which service is required. Staff are rarely in evidence as a result. The economical and brilliant electric lighting was a feature common in Chicago retail premises at that time, but was considered an innovation in a London house. The heating from the furnace room also, which avoids entirely the dust and dirt and noise and unwanted labour of coal and ashes in the house – a hot-water system it is, admirable for the time it was put in, and ensuring that the house is kept at a constant temperature throughout. All the rooms have either deadened floors or doubled ceilings, or both. The quality of solemn tranquillity which this gives to it has often been noted, making Brooke Street a welcome haven of quiet amidst the sea of this great city's noise.

Within this noble and effective setting we had determined that the house should be full of beautiful things, and the primary purpose of the whole should be the expression of all that was beautiful, good and lively in the daily routine of its owners. What journeys many of the objects which now furnish these rooms have made! Many of the most precious had adorned our first home, and having crossed the ocean once when we had carried them with us on our return from our first visits to Europe, now crossed it again. Chief amongst them were the carpets and furnishings, made to antique designs by Morris and Company, augmented with precious oriental originals; also the lustre tiles of the dining-room fireplace, in a design first purchased from Louis C. Tiffany on State Street and then repeated in lighting fixtures and table-ware since purchased from the same firm, now also trading at number twenty-two Regent Street.

You must not think, for all the commercial detail given in this account, that the creation of these rooms was lightly done; each purchase was most carefully made. The golden glass of the hall-way door, for instance, adapted from that in my father's house, of which Mr Richardson had heard me speak, produces a light admirably in harmony with the darkened and polished oak used here and throughout the house as panelling. The Turkey stair-carpet and the dark rose African marble on which Mr Richardson insisted for the mantel of the hall fireplace complete the overall impression, which is then given life and fire by the iridescent glasswork of Tiffany, Galli and Pauly here so prominently dis-played. This effect is then repeated throughout all the family rooms in lustreware, oriental lacquer and brasswork, all of such finish and polish that the absence of firelight, so often the source of liveliness in an interior, is rarely remarked on. The warmth and light of this house, indeed its very spirit, comes from its careful arrangement. An example: the set of eight chairs in the dining-room – the head-chair of which you may yourself occupy on your coming of age – were made to complement the grandest of the family pieces, the great veneered table made by my own Grandfather, and handed down ever since. It stands, at Mr Richardson's suggestion, at the exact conjunction of the Brooke Street and Gilbert Street axes of the house, and is thus its true heart and centre. It was around this table that the family gathered to celebrate the marriage of your Mother and your Father on that happy afternoon in February 1900, and it is to this table that the guests of the house are still summoned.

Of note among the lesser furnishings that have helped to make the house what it is are the family portraits, and a small collection of photographic reproductions of the works of the European mas-ters. These I mention since they may easily be overlooked or dismissed, framed as they are in the somewhat over-elaborate style of the eighties; yet they are precious to me as souvenirs of our very first travels on this continent in the spring following our marriage. They include my own particular favourite, Rubens' *Descent from the Cross* purchased from the magnificent new museum of Antwerp, and also an *Arrival at Bethlehem* chosen from amongst the Bruegels in Brussels. The snow scenes of this master are an especial taste of your Grandmother's, and this particular subject is much in my mind as I write this, reminding me as it does not only of the various journeys I have myself undertaken but also of what I take to be a great and sacred principle, namely that all journeys must come to rest in a home, no matter where that home be situated. Even that Holy couple, depicted by the Flemish master journeying through snow in this enactment of their story, must seek out the House that is their desired destination.

Much comment was made in the year of the house's completion as to its oddity and severity. The massive entrance arch, seeming almost to hide the Brooke Street doorway, was much discussed. It is true that it gives little hint of the hospitality afforded to those invited into the rooms which lie on the other side of the heavy oak door. With the passing of time familiarity has perhaps softened what once seemed strange; but still, I am glad to say, those who look closely at the house will observe that above the barred and obscured front door are the family initials, carved in still unweathered stone in Mr Richardson's grandest and most permanent "Romanesque" style; a proud commitment publicly made by its first owners to every detail of their house.

I had not realised how many and how various are its features until I began to catalogue them in my mind; each one, it seems, carries a story which can only be deciphered by one acquainted with its origins. The best I can do is to offer this imperfect record, together with these photographs, to perpetuate or at least suggest their spirit. The home was ever a haven of rest. It was no easy task to make it so. We trust you will keep it, and keep it as it was intended to be, at such time as it becomes yours to live in.

Perhaps you and those who come after you may be interested to look this record over when lacking better occupation. I would have you realise that it is more a catalogue than a history, and sadly deficient as either, but it may still serve to recall some experiences of your own youth, and to lead in your imagination to some consideration of the times your forebears had here.

C. Beauchamp Vail, London, 1910

Excerpt from *"The Making of a House: The Story of Eighteen Brooke Street"*. Ms. dedicated in author's hand *"For my Grandson"*. Ms CBV 46.11, Vail papers, *Victoria and Albert Museum. Quoted with permission.*

Christmas Eve

Just put my holly sprigs up over the picture.

Got the radio on. Lovely.

Spending Christmas on your own isn't so bad. In fact, it's good. When I get home on a Friday (in an ordinary week) the thing which is supposed to be the worst, the not having anyone to talk to, is the best, actually. After all those questions and answers all day every day for five days I'm ready for it. So this is my idea of real luxury; not just Saturday and Sunday but Saturday, Sunday, Monday *and* Tuesday. Saturday and Sunday off as usual – I sometimes think that is the reason why I put the backs up of the Misses Elton in Haberdashery and Cosmetics, Banking being the only department in the House that doesn't work on a Saturday – Saturday and Sunday off as usual, then tomorrow Christmas Day, Tuesday Boxing, back in for the sale preparations on Wednesday.

But that's Wednesday, and tonight's Sunday.

And every hour precious, I can tell you, after the week I've had. After the year I've had actually. I know it's not over yet, but I can't say I shall mind when it is. Over and done with. Too many mornings sitting there on the number twenty-nine and catching sight of things in the papers over people's shoulders. Not on the front pages, of course, but there all the same on page five or six. For public consumption. On far too many mornings for just the one year. It hasn't been easy.

Snow soon apparently.

I should be laying the table by now I suppose (I always like to do it the night before), clearing this away. But no one's watching me, there's nobody much out on the street, nobody's likely to look up here at the fifth floor window and wonder if I've got everything ready yet, are they? I can sit here at the table until one o'clock in the morning if I want to.

Voices do carry on the stairs of this building but not the sounds inside the rooms. Certainly not the sound of someone writing.

Anyway, I've got the radio on. I've got the gas on and I've got the radio on and I've got no plans at all.

That's one of the worst things about the weeks before Christmas, as if the extra customers weren't bad enough, being obliged to hear discussion of everybody's Plans. Plans For The Festive Season. I've had Miss Elton Haberdashery and Miss Elton Cosmetics going on and on in the lift every single morning this week, it made me feel just like Miss Johnson in that awful scene in the train when Dolly Messiter can't stop talking and all Miss Johnson wants to do is have a quiet think about Trevor Howard and die. I know just how she feels. First thing in the morning; trains and snow, snow and trains, "We'll all be together I expect if Anne can get down from Watford on the last train all right, I just hope it doesn't get too bad, did you read that forecast? I know it's lovely to wake up on the morning itself and have it all white for the children but you know how unreliable the Metropolitan can be if it gets too heavy." And then of course you know what's coming next; "On your own again this year, Mr Page, I expect?", always said very sympathetically of course, very concerned.

I don't think I could stand for it if I thought they did actually feel sorry for me. I think I would have to say something. As it is, all they ever get is, "Yes, that's right Miss Elton." Yes, that's right, Miss Elton Haberdashery. "On my own again this year," said with just the right touch of bitterness, which of course they find all highly satisfactory. Oh they do like you to know that they know all about your being single at your age. ("That Mr Page in Banking got up on the wrong side of the bed this morning, Miss Elton." "And on the wrong side of fifty, from the look of him, on the wrong side of fifty at the very least Miss Elton.")

Last year I cooked the whole dinner anyway, just to spite them. All day it took me. Everything; the chipolatas, the redcurrant jelly, the Cumberland sauce, the smallest bird in London. The whole business. Laying the table the night before, drinking the whole bottle myself, carving for myself, telling myself that I deserved it after the year I'd had and then hardly eating a thing. Sitting here and letting it all go cold. All that business of getting it ready and then all the work of clearing up, but nothing in between. Just sitting there in my chair by the gas staring at the picture with the two sprigs of holly up over it. All those people in the snow.

I think that was what made me not want to do all that again this year, looking at the picture one evening last week and reminding myself to get the holly sprigs and realising that I was going to be doing exactly what Miss Elton Cosmetics imagines me doing when she says that, "On your own again this year I expect Mr Page?" Oh yes, she can just imagine it. *A grown man cooking his own Christmas dinner, well it's sad really isn't it, she can just imagine him sitting there in his Saturday suit with his paper crown from a cracker that he's pulled by himself, no but we shouldn't laugh, not really. It must be so sad knowing that's how they'll end up, don't you think? Of course there was that couple in number eleven, but in the end of course it's bound to happen, wouldn't you say, Miss Elton? I certainly would, Miss Elton. I certainly would.*

And of course she would, because that's what I've always told them, "Yes, on my own again this year, Miss Elton." That's what I told them and they believed me.

So this year I said to myself, on Thursday, when I was on my way in on the number twenty-nine, I'm not going to bother with any of it. Except the drink. Sherry before, claret with, brandy for the butter, rum for the sauce, scotch in the afternoon, a few beers with the sandwiches in the evening. Four days and eleven bottles. I do things all the year round that they can't possibly imagine me doing, not that nice Mr Page from Banking, and so I'm not going to turn all predictable just because it's the twenty-fourth of December. Catch me hurrying home to start my Festive Preparations, I thought. Catch me hurrying home like it was *A Christmas Carol* or something. Like I was one of the people in the picture.

I have got the holly sprigs up though. Got them on Wellington Street Market on Friday. I do like the market when they have all the lights on over the stalls, the lemons and the mistletoe bunches and the greenery and everybody shouting and of course all those boys on the stalls taking liberties on a Friday night. The things they shout out at you sometimes. That one boy, the one with the forearms who works on the greengrocers by the petshop, he's the worst. Cheeky. Giving me the whistle when he sees me coming. But I can tell he knows of course really I love it, "And what can I do for you, sir," he says. Cheeky sod.

After I'd got the bottles, one more bag was all I could carry, so I just got a bit of whatever I fancied, and when the bag was full the holly sprigs went on top and that was it. Which is not like me at all. Usually I would have worked out exactly what I needed to get me through till Wednesday. Me and my routines. In and out on the number twenty-nine every morning and evening, Monday to Friday, then Friday night, Wellington Street Market, three bags of groceries. Early night. Jermyn Street on Saturday, and sometimes a picture in Leicester Square. Not much on Sunday, iron a shirt for the morning, early night. Well, it will do me good to forget exactly what I've got in for tomorrow's supper just this once. Do me good to forget. Forget where I've put things.

I'm fifty-three, you see, and I know exactly where everything is.

So this year, the holly sprigs are it. Your lot. Not surprising that I'm not much of a one for decorations is it, really. I get enough of those, working on Oxford Street. Clowns it was last year, soldiers the year before. This year we've got Santa Claus going right across the front of the store with twenty-two Christmas trees and giant snow-flakes that light up at half-past three in the afternoon. Nice for the kids who get brought to see the windows but lacking any real style I should say, not like the decorations before the war. And what with the crowds this year, it's a wonder anyone can see anything anyway.

Funny, even though I'm not doing any of the preparations, I've still got all those Christmas Eve feelings that you get no matter what, and I do want it to snow. I couldn't remember the last time that it had actually happened, a real White Christmas, but they've just said on the radio when the last one was. I wouldn't have remembered the date unless they had said it. Christmas of 1923.

It's been coming for quite a while now. Freezing it was when I was out yesterday. I considered the Biograph or perhaps a matinée somewhere, but I thought I'd stick to Jermyn Street as always. Such a creature of habit, the shop-girl. Funny to think about it, us all sitting there while the rest of London's freezing. It made me laugh when I was coming home, everyone heading down to Regent Street for the last minute shopping, heads down, wanting to get in out of the cold, slipping and sliding with all their parcels (you never realise how much a street slopes until the ice comes) and none of them having any idea that a bit further down and turn right there's all the regulars in Jermyn Street sitting stark naked like a row of orchids in a steamed-up greenhouse. All us old boys sitting there in the steam like giant pink orchids, discussing whether it's really going to turn to snow like we've been promised. I gave myself a good three hours yesterday, a proper lather, a proper treat, and then I was straight across the street all wrapped up pink and clean and lovely before the cold had a real chance to get at me. Into Speke and Sons opposite. Finally bought myself that dressing-gown I've been admiring in their window every Saturday afternoon for the last six months. Of course I got the look from the assistant, me not being the sort of gentleman he usually serves, he made that quite clear. I wanted to say to him, don't you give me any of your Yes-sir-and-were-you-looking-for-anything-in-particular manners, I know all about them. I've been in retail since before you were born.

They do do a grey gentleman's dressing-gown in the Bargain Basement at work, of course, the so-called Less Expensive Range, meaning Cheap, and I could have got it even cheaper if I'd waited and braved the crowds on Wednesday; but it wouldn't be the same grey and it wouldn't be silk and it wouldn't have the hand-rolled butter-yellow piping. And it wouldn't be from Jermyn Street. It wouldn't be what I've been promising myself all year. I know when something is quality and when it isn't; and not just because I've been working in a shop for thirty-eight years. I've only ever put quality things next to my body. That's the thing that makes Jermyn Street such a treat, and a rare treat too, these days; the whole street is quality, from the back door of Simpson's right along to Upper Regent Street. Nobody's making do with the jacket they bought to stand and watch the Coronation go past. Nobody's tarting themselves up with a pair of tight trousers, not on Jermyn Street. No Brylcreem down there; it's all very Gentleman's Pomade. Ivory-backed brushes and ivory-handled razors (matching). Real badger. Handmade shirts with the studs all laid out in sets in their pigskin cases. Gold links (what were his? Sapphires) and English Fern Eau de Cologne. What with the London and Provincial Turkish at number seventy-six you've got everything you could ever want to touch your skin right there on the one street. Everything a Gentleman needs. Something to fit him exactly, something to scrape and smooth and scent and shine him and brush him and dress him right up. Everything he needs to keep his body feeling exactly the same as it feels the minute after you've finished the steam and the plunge and then got dressed and walked out into the cold.

It feels new. That's it. New.

And yours. You really feel your body is yours.

I did get it out of the bag and give it a try on when I got it home but now I think I'm going to wrap it up, wrap it up and give it to myself in the morning, just like a real Christmas present. And then tomorrow I'm going to have the gas on all day and I'm going to sit here with my radio on and my grey paisley-printed silk with the butter-yellow and my bottles and nobody else here. Just like a real gentleman.

I shan't bother to wrap these notebooks up though – I don't know why I bought myself three of them. It wasn't as a present – it was at least a month ago and I wasn't even really thinking about Christmas then. I never kept a diary and I don't know why I'm

Except this isn't a diary really.

They do say that this week between Christmas and the New Year is the week to sort things out, don't they, though it seems to me that what with the Last Minute Rush so-called, and then the Festivities, and then the Sales, most people spend the week avoiding doing just that. I never wanted to write anything down and I don't know why I should now. Odd the radio mentioning the White Christmas like that. Thirty-three years.

·····

Now it's Tchaikovsky, the "Enchanter's Song" from *Swan Lake*. Lovely, lovely. Down they come, on to the black water, before it ices over completely. Whiter than the snow. Gas on, bottle open.

I've just been to the window, and here it comes. Snow in the darkness at five o'clock almost exactly, Christmas Eve 1956. Snow covering everything, the bombsites, the rooftops, the decorations, the top of the number twenty-nine when it gets stuck at the lights outside the Dominion, Oxford Street, Wellington Street, the Park, the pavements, the papers, the names, the addresses, all the rest, everything. The whole bloody year. The whole bloody thing. The whole bloody situation.

   I don't sleep terribly well at the moment anyway. So I may as well have another drink and then I'm going to start.

The first time I ever went to number eighteen Brooke Street it was in the snow.

Does that sound like a proper first sentence?

"I opened the window and could hear the muffled roar of Park Lane from beyond my quiet street." – I like that one, except that obviously I wouldn't open the window in this weather, not at this time in the evening. And actually there was no roar in those days, there being very little traffic in comparison to now. And of course you could hear Park Lane from Brooke Street, that's obvious, but you can't hear it from here.

"He seemed at first sight quite an ordinary man" – which I can still remember without even having to look it up, having read that opening paragraph four times straight away, coming straight back here from the man who had got it in for me on the Charing Cross Road and starting it even before eating. That was the first time I had ever read a book about

A book like that. And of course the best one, well it's certainly still my favourite, is probably "Last night I dreamt I went to Manderley again", which I've always loved, and that's exactly the sort of effect I should like to begin with. The way that just those words can send you up that overgrown driveway again, twisting and turning through the rhododendron bushes (of course the music in the film is wonderful, that helps). And you know just from those first words that you're going to see the house again, and you're going to find out what happened there, and even though you know already, you shiver, because you're going to find out all over again.

The first time I ever went to number eighteen Brooke Street it was in the snow.

Five times, I went to number eighteen Brooke Street; and the
first time, it was snowing.

I can remember that I had gone home and changed into my
other suit, so I must have thought it was going to be a special
occasion even before I got there – after all, I could easily have
walked straight round there after work in two minutes if I had
wanted to.

It was my first Christmas alone in London. It was only two
days before I had stood in front of the letter-box outside the
Camden Town tube station and closed my eyes and taken a deep
breath, and finally posted the letter telling them that I wouldn't
be coming home that year. I didn't have any special plans, apart
from the party at work, but I was going to be on my own, in
London, in a room of my own, and that was special enough.

Then, when I was asked out to somebody's house like that,
well you can imagine how excited I must have been. I had never
been to a house in Mayfair before – that whole world south of
Oxford Street was a mystery to me.

I turned left down Gilbert Street, and put all the noise and
the crowds behind me. And there on the corner it was, tall
and dark and red. I didn't go straight to the front door; I crossed
over Brooke Street and stood under the street lamp and took a
good look at it.

Number eighteen looked very dark and strange that night, not
at all what I was expecting, and indeed number eighteen was
not at all like any of the other houses on Brooke Street. For a
start, it was built of stone, not brick, and when you first saw it,
there on the corner of Gilbert Street, it seemed to be rising up
over you, even though it was actually only four storeys high. The
other houses were all dark too, shuttered. One, two doors down,
had cars pulling up outside, and suddenly there were smart
women in fur getting out and making a dash through the snow,
shrieking with laughter, as if being out in the night air was some
sort of a joke, dashing up the front steps and into the hallway,
so that I got a quick glimpse of the chandeliers inside that had
been lit to welcome them. Evening dress and big cars, I suppose
that's what I had thought number eighteen would be like. But at

number eighteen all there was was the one dim pane of glass barely glowing behind the bars on the door, so that you weren't sure if your eyes had deceived you. So that I wasn't at all sure if there was anyone home or not.

The snow had just begun to settle, outlining the great red blocks of stone, making it look more like a castle or prison than a house. And it seemed older than the other houses somehow.

I stopped for a moment on the steps and watched how the snow turned gold as it fell through the light coming from the barred window; then I took off my hat and cleared my throat and rang the bell. I wondered if the sound inside would be electric, or actually a bell ringing – I could just imagine the sound of a bell echoing down a dark, empty corridor, because those were the kind of things that the outside of number eighteen made you imagine at night. Even though you knew you were right in the middle of London you felt you could have been standing at the gates of Manderley, or that you were Beauty lifting the great brass knocker and hearing the noise echo through the Beast's lair. Little Red Riding Hood standing outside the cottage with the snow settling on her hair and wondering why it was all so quiet, wondering why Grandmother was taking so long to answer the door.

The first thing that struck you was the heat. That, and the fact that even standing on the doorstep you could see the kind of money he had. The great flight of polished stairs rising into the darkness at the end of the hallway, the bunches of bronze and glass lilies set into the panelled wall; the fireplace, the high shelf of expensive-looking plates and vases. Talk about another world.

It was a butler who opened the door – or I assume it was a butler. I never saw him again after that first visit. I stood there holding my hat, and trying not to look too out of place. The heat from the house was melting the snow on me. I said who I was, and that I thought I was expected, but the butler didn't seem at all sure. He seemed very put out – angry, I'd have said. Angry at something – and I assumed it was at me, of course. He asked me to wait, and then left me standing there. After he had disappeared back into the depths of the house he must have turned a switch; suddenly the glass lilies came alight all along the whole length of the hall, and up on the first landing. With the lights on, I could see that there were no signs of any preparations for a party, and that there were no hats (I was still holding mine) hanging on the hat-stand, and no umbrellas in the giant Japanese vase by the door. There was no fire in the fireplace. Everything was – well, everything looked like a museum at closing time. I couldn't hear any sound at all.

And so of course I was off at once blaming myself for coming. *Why on earth should a man like that have asked me to his house for Christmas Eve, we hardly knew each other* – and I expect I started blushing, standing there in my Saturday suit and still holding my hat, feeling like a fool because I hadn't even been asked to take my coat off. Telling myself I should have known that the whole idea of him even saying to someone like me *oh do come round to my house* in that beautiful, loud Mayfair voice he had was a joke anyway, I should have seen that.

I stood there in the empty hall for what seemed like minutes, with no idea how to behave, turning my hat brim in my hands. Me and my first Christmas Eve in London. Blushing like a beet. I always have been quick to blush. Blood everywhere, my mother used to say.

And that was the exact moment when I saw that wonderful hair for the very first time.

When I first saw it I didn't realise what it was – I thought it was a bird, I don't know why; the wings of a bird, something white, trapped in the house, trying to escape. I hadn't heard anything, and he just, well, he just appeared, there at the top of the hall stairs. Even in the heavy gold light of the lilies, his hair was pure white – white like a magician's dove; or like the swans when they settle on the black water. He hadn't seen me yet. For a moment he hesitated, as if unsure which of the several doors on the landing he had been heading for – and then he did see me. He looked as though he'd been – caught. He stared at me for just a moment, and then started to come across the landing. As he came towards the top of the stairs I thought from the look on his face that he was going to ask me a question – but not "Can I help you?" or "Can I take your hat, Sir"; for some reason I had the strongest impression that he was going to ask me something, had I seen something he'd lost, could I tell him the time – I don't know, something like that. Then his face clouded; I think he saw my hat and coat and realised that I must be a guest, not another member of the staff. He hesitated again, and at that point there was a shout, coming from somewhere deep in the house on the ground floor – and when I looked back up to the landing the young man with the white hair had disappeared. He had hardly had time to open and close one of the doors on the landing – they looked heavy, mahogany – surely I would have heard the noise of him doing it. It was as if he had simply walked through one of the walls.

I told myself I must have imagined the shouting.

As I waited, I began to notice what everyone must have noticed about the house, apart from the heat; everything in it seemed to shine. All those glass vases and plates. If they had been flowers, you'd have said that they grew best in the shade; deadly night-shade. The bronze stems of the lilies, the gold glass shades, the marble of the fireplace, the fireplace tiles with their design of red and gold vines and thistles, the big Japanese vase, the dark wood of the walls and the stairs, the banister rails (almost black with polish), the brass rods holding down the stair-carpet, the frames of the pictures hung in close rows on the landing walls – every-thing was catching light from somewhere, shining. Gleaming. Because it was so quiet, and because people kept on disappearing, I began to have a notion that this was one of those magic houses you used to get in children's stories, where the doors are opened and the meals served and all the things get polished by invisible hands. I began to wonder how old it all was. Perhaps it had all been shut up in the dark like this for years and years.

Now I definitely could hear shouting; a door slammed some-where upstairs, someone was running to an upper room – but then the butler came back, and he didn't give me any chance to ask for an explanation for anything. He said he was very sorry, but the party had had to be cancelled and would I please accept the mas-ter's apologies. Of course I would, I said. I did up my coat, I put my hat back on, and I went. I was quite glad to, actually.

From the moment that he had opened the front door for me to the moment that he showed me out it had been quite clear that he had absolutely no idea who I was or why I was there.

Now, I wouldn't put up with that sort of behaviour at all. I wouldn't say anything, of course, but that would certainly be the last time that I had anything to do with them. But back then, you see, I was very much at everybody's beck and call. I was still very much the junior at work, having only just started in the Department. In those days it was still always "Would you help this gentleman please Mr Page?" – "Certainly Sir, good afternoon Sir; and how can I help you?" – that was me. The young one, the plain-looking one, eager to please. They trained you to be very deferential to all the customers, but especially to any customer who was what you might call posh or who had a good address. Which Brooke Street West One certainly was – and still is. You can always tell, and not just from their address or their voice. Their skin is different – that's always what I notice first with the real gentlemen.

And so no wonder I was on my best behaviour in the hallway of number eighteen. Beholding. And also, you see, at that age and at that address I had no way of telling how I was being treated; for all I knew that was the way that a servant in a house like that was meant to talk, and especially to a person like me. And even when I had been walking there I had already half been expecting something like this, so that as I was putting my hat back on I was telling myself *that's all right, no, of course, certainly, sir*; of course he hadn't really meant it, of course he hadn't really meant it when he had looked straight at me like that as bold as you like and said, "Do come, I'd like to . . . I'd like to – meet you." That hadn't been what he had meant at all

And so I didn't ask the butler what was wrong; I didn't ask him if there was anything happening upstairs that I wasn't supposed to know about; I didn't ask him what was the real reason why I was being sent away again, I just said that was no trouble at all, and that I would hope to see Mr Clive on another occasion (that's what I always called him, or rather that's how I've always thought of him, although Clive isn't his surname; Master Clive. Master of the house). I said I hoped to see him on some other occasion and then I went back home to spend my Christmas Eve on my own. Went home on the bus. In the snow, in my best suit.

And that's always how I remember number eighteen; somewhere where they invite you round, but never let you in. Dark and silent, and hot even when it's snowing. No wonder I think it's Manderley. No wonder I dreamt last night I went there again.

And that's always how I remember the stairs at number eighteen, looking up and catching a sudden flash of white hair in the darkness, a bird's wing.

That snow's really coming down now.

of course he didn't know where he was going, the first time that I saw him, because at that time on Christmas Eve he had probably only been in Mr Clive's employ some two hours at most. Of course he didn't know where all the doors were or which one to go through

··············

People who don't live here always say that the thing about London is that you never bump into anyone by accident. And certainly I can remember the feeling of walking down Piccadilly or Oxford Street when I first got here, and thinking, no one knows me; no one in all this crowd knows me. But the way that I met Mr Clive B. Vivian shows you that that isn't always the case.

It was almost two months before Christmas that it happened, early November I should say – that's if you don't count the first time I saw him. It was only on the second occasion that I actually spoke to him, you see – the time that I did, literally, bump into him. It was my usual time for Jermyn Street – I say usual, I suppose in fact at that time I was only just beginning to go; the West End was a whole new world for someone like me, and the London and Provincial Turkish was part of it that I'd only just discovered. Anyway it must have been a Saturday afternoon, because that has always been when I've gone, and I was on the pavement just outside the door of the baths. I was just putting my gloves on – it was cold – and I must admit that I wasn't looking where I was going. There was another man, somebody who I

Somebody who I thought I recognised, and I was watching

him walk up Jermyn Street towards the Haymarket; and when he reached the corner he looked back over his shoulder at me, and then obviously I looked away, because I didn't want anyone thinking that I was staring at them, certainly not a stranger, because it wasn't as if it was anyone I knew, he was a stranger, I'd never seen him before in my life – and then this other gentleman walked smack into me and nearly knocked me over. Which was Mr Clive B. Vivian. *C.B.V.*, as it said in the stone up over the door of number eighteen. Although I didn't know that yet.

We both almost fell – the pavement was icy. He grabbed me by the shoulders to stop us from going over, and I must have grabbed his arm with the hand that had no glove on it, because I could feel that his coat was real cashmere – and through the sleeve I could feel how hard his arm was. We ended up face to face, with our arms round each other. Which is an odd way for two men to meet. Just for a moment we were looking right into each other's eyes. With our breath rising and mixing between us. You do see these little accidents happening when the pavements are icy like that.

I said, "Excuse me", or whatever, and he said, "Jesus", which I remember quite distinctly. He didn't have an accent, but he did sometimes say things the American way like that. You noticed it, because otherwise everything about him and his voice was very much the gentleman, as if someone had gone and ordered the whole effect from one of the Complete Outfitters. Sometimes this other voice would come out and you would wonder what he was actually like, I mean what he was like at home on his own, when he took off those wonderful suits that he always wore.

He was obviously in a hurry; there was just a moment when we were standing there face to face holding each other up and then he let go of me and turned up his collar and walked smartly off down towards Simpson's without any sort of comment, much less apology. So that I didn't have time to say that I had seen him the week before.

But I had; exactly the week before, and at exactly the same time, just as I was coming out of the baths. Obviously he didn't remember being there, or rather he didn't remember seeing me there. Well, there was no reason why he should.

There wasn't anything odd about me being on the same street at the same time two Saturdays in a row, because that was when I went to the baths, but it did strike me as odd that he should be there. I mean, you notice these things, don't you? You – well, you get to know pretty quick that if somebody doesn't have a good reason to be standing around then there is only one good reason for them to be standing around. If you see what I mean.

I would have put it all down to coincidence, or at least have just said to myself, *don't ask* – he obviously wasn't somebody you could just go up to on this street and ask – but when on the very next Saturday I came out at half-past four and there he was again, on the pavement opposite this time, well I had to say something, didn't I?

Sometimes people do resort to being "accidentally" in the same place at the same time as you, but that was hardly something that a gentleman like him would resort to doing. So I didn't know quite what to make of it when I saw him standing there looking into a shop window. I could see that he'd positioned himself at just the right angle so that he would get a good view of anyone coming out of the baths, reflected in the glass; I wasn't that green. When you come out of the Turkish, you feel very calm, and very private. I don't know what it is; something to do with the way you can still feel your skin under your clothes, and something to do with the way that in there, people see you from the neck down, and I have always looked good from the neck down, and when they see me more or less naked like that nobody looks at me and sees Mr Page, I mean Mr Page, Banking, Monday to Friday. And so when you come out into the real world again, out on to Jermyn Street and down on to the Haymarket, you want to hold on to that feeling for a while. You feel – you still feel naked, that's it. Naked in the street in London West One. That's right, Officer, if you don't mind. And so as I say when I saw him there, for the third time, staring at me, I didn't know how to take it. I didn't know what he knew about me.

He was the first one to speak; as soon as he spotted me he crossed the street and came right up to me. "Well, at least we've managed not to walk into each other this time. Do you come here quite often?"

"Yes, I do – " I said –

"How odd; so do I. That's my tailor just across the street. Three damned fittings I've had for this one, three Saturday afternoons in a row gone, still, at least the bloody thing's finished. They said they'd send it round but quite frankly after all that I felt like wearing it home – what do you think?"

I felt such a fool. He did look splendid. You notice these things on a gentleman – or I do. The way a suit fits exactly. You can never get that except by always having them made by the same tailor, someone who really knows your build. Not just how you stand but how you move, that's the trick. Especially across the shoulders. A very dark grey stripe and four buttons it was, under a cashmere overcoat. And his gloves; hardly anyone would wear yellow gloves in town now, and certainly not of that quality.

He wasn't asking my opinion because he was unsure. He knew what he looked like, they always do. If he had been a customer then we would have said that he was very forward.

"And what's your excuse?"

I explained about the London and Provincial, which he said he didn't know about. Then he asked me if they were "any good". I was quite careful when he asked me that, and said well, yes, they were, and that you could get a massage, and so on. I couldn't work out if he really wanted to know or if he was just making conversation, or if

Then he asked me if I always went there at the same time and I said that well, yes, I did, every Saturday, at the same time.

We didn't exchange names or anything, and I wasn't quite sure that I – well, there was something about the way that Mr Clive looked at you. He looked straight at you, and he made it seem as though you should be answering a question, giving an account of yourself, taking the hint, as if he was always thinking *Yes, yes, come on, I haven't got all day*. And I didn't know – well, I didn't know why he was talking to me. I mean, if you had seen us in the street together, face to face, then you might well have wondered what on earth we had to talk about like that, because it was obvious from the way that we were dressed that we were very different types of people. We were on different sides of the counter, so to speak. He was having his suit made to measure in

Jermyn Street and mine was from Menswear, first floor; he was coming out of his tailor's and turning right towards Simpson's and St James's, and I was going to go left and walk all the way up to the Dominion and catch the number twenty-nine. You might have wondered what on earth we could have had in common.

But if you overlooked the way we were dressed, then of course, well, it was obvious what we had in common. I noticed it straight away, even the first time.

Because you see Mr Clive and I looked the same. Exactly.

As I said, I can remember him looking me right in the eye; that was because we were the same height, to the inch. We were both dark-haired, both very clear-skinned (well we were both twenty). Stocky rather than slim. And when we were face to face you might well have thought, stick my hat and suit on him and you could have sent him to work in the Department; put his suit on me and maybe I could even have passed in the restaurant at Simpson's, with a little practice. Mr Clive was black-haired and plain-faced in exactly the same way that I am; neither of us had what you could call "looks". Neither of us was the sort of twenty-year-old to make heads turn on the street, although in the London and Provincial I certainly got the looks, and still do sometimes. Some people have even told me that I should go into competition, with my back and arms. I'm still in better shape than most of them, to my eyes anyway. Mr Clive had at least as good a shape as I did – you can't carry a build like ours off unless you're really trim.

All the time we were talking, I could see the two of us reflected in the shop window opposite. If we'd ever gone to the baths together, if we'd sat on opposite benches in the steam room for instance, or if we'd lathered up or oiled up together, we would have been twins. In those days, of course, you had to have a good eye to see how somebody was built under their clothes – there weren't any of these American shirts rolled up over the bicep, or these "blue-jeans" showing everything. Well I could always tell, I notice these things. I don't know if he was in shape naturally or if he had had to work for it – it can be either at that age. I certainly had it naturally then, although I have had to work hard at it since. Exercises in the bedroom first thing, the staff Gymnasium three times a week, the dumb-bells, a good proper stiff walk from Tottenham Court Road right down Oxford Street to the House every week-day morning no matter what the weather, and of course a good sweat and a plunge in the baths every Saturday. And I always oil myself when I get home; that's an important part of keeping the look at my age. Get the fire on, put a towel on the carpet, and have a good oil up. The light from the gold silk lampshades and the bottle of whisky on the sideboard for when you feel like one. The gas on full so that you're never cold in the bedroom either, I can't stand all that hiding under the sheets. Fine sheets they are too. Not what you would necessarily expect to find in a flat like this, as several people have commented on in their time. Not what you would expect from Mr Page, Banking. Oh yes, quite a taste for the finer things in life.

The finer things in life. Alike in more than just build, Mr Clive and I were.

He always ended his conversations as suddenly as he started them; he'd wait for just a moment to see if you had anything to say for yourself (that was when you got that sense of him thinking, *Yes, yes; well?*), and then he'd supply your answer for you; "In that case," he said, "perhaps we might bump into each other again one day," and he laughed. He had a way of laughing to himself like that, as if a lot of things in life were private jokes for him. I think I asked him if he was going to be coming back for another suit.

"No," he said, "no. That won't be why I'll be coming back."

And then there was one of his pauses, where he looked at you and expected you to ask why, but it was too short for you to actually say anything, and only just long enough for him to raise one eyebrow so that you knew he was thinking, *Well, Mr Page, I haven't got all day you know* –

"Cufflinks. Yes, that's it. Cufflinks. I think I might come back for some cufflinks. And if it happens to be half-past four on a Saturday afternoon, well; well then we might just see each other again. You never can tell."

Just the sort of usual stilted conversation you have on the street if you don't really know someone, I suppose. If you had passed us on the pavement then you might have wondered what I had to look so embarrassed about. I never have got any better at that sort of thing.

Supposing somebody did read this.

But on the other hand, if they knew what it meant, then they wouldn't tell anyone else, because then they'd have to explain how and why they knew.

That's all right then.

And if they don't know, then it doesn't matter. You could stand in the middle of this carpet and look round this flat and take a good look at every single thing I've got here and still have absolutely no idea. You could open all the doors. You could even stand in the doorway of my bedroom and have a good old stare at my bed with the heavy linen sheets and you'd have absolutely no idea. For instance people often say, "Oh I know just how you feel", and I always think, oh no you don't, you don't have any idea at all of how it feels. That's how it all works, isn't it; knowing, and not knowing. If you've seen someone inside the baths, then of course when you meet them outside you are bound to be a bit wary, you may not be sure exactly how to start the conversation (some people are bolder, but not me), but at least you know where you are, and I don't mean just knowing what they looked like in the changing room, though of course that helps. You know. You know how it could feel half an hour from now or however long it takes to get back to where he lives or to some place that he knows. And after all, it is Saturday, it is your day off. For instance that man I mentioned, that other man on Jermyn Street, the "somebody who I thought I knew", well that wasn't it at all. Of course I bloody knew. Even in the changing room we were looking at each other. And then in the steam room I had to cover myself with my hands because it was showing. I knew all right. And when you know like that, well then you time getting changed so that you leave more or less together (not actually together, obviously) and all the time you're thinking, perhaps he has somewhere to go, and then you get out on to Jermyn Street and if it was nowadays of course you'd be thinking perhaps he'll go on to the Coffeehouse on the Haymarket, and I can sit at his table and get him talking – but back then there wasn't anywhere convenient to go like that, so you'd have to do all that "not really looking" business, pretending to stop and put your gloves on so that you could see if he was stopping at the corner, and of course this one did, and he turned, and he grinned, which was very bold. I love it when they do that. And I know I should have just grinned back and got on with it, but being me of course I had to stall a bit and look away, I suppose I never want to quite admit – and then bang, somebody grabs me from behind by both shoulders.

I thought it was the law.

Of course I thought it was the law.

I thought that somebody had been watching me and could tell what I was thinking and that they knew and that I'd had it; straight away I thought that. I'm always ready to think that.

Always right ready with an explanation, Officer, you know me. You'll say I'm jumpy, well of course I'm jumpy, I read the papers, don't I? It may be tucked away on page five or six but it still makes you jumpy. Male Nurse, Actor Arrested – not that he was well known or anything – and then that other one who was, who certainly was well known, three months ago (I thought he was marvellous in that show at the Haymarket), giving himself a false name, describing himself as a clerk with an income of £500 a year, how on earth did he ever imagine – well, they do all pile up, these cases, don't they, Officer? –

"And just remind us where it was that you said that you first met him, sir?"

"Jermyn Street, Officer. Saturday the – "

"Ah yes so it was sir . . . just wanted to make sure that we'd all got our details in order sir . . ." And then (there are always two of them, aren't there, in the films), and then the other one, the younger one, he's been leaning against the wall on the other side of the room with his arms crossed, he comes over and gives you a cigarette and lights it for you, and then of course you get all the "Look you might as well tell us sir" routine.

"You might as well tell us, sir. Had you known him long? Did you" (and this is where he leans right over the desk so that his face is too close to yours, and the light is too bright, and you're tired, you've been over all this again and again) *"did you know him well, sir?"*.

And so on.

Got to get all the details right, you see. Get it all laid out nicely before I go to bed. Not getting the details right is like speaking ill of the dead.

And if somebody did read that last bit, if they did recognise all the details, and if they decided that they did know what I'd been doing, if they did work out what I'd actually been thinking, what I'd been up to, well, it's all thirty odd years ago now isn't it?

Thirty-three actually, Officer Maguire.

Anyway I told Mr Clive that if he did come back for his cufflinks then yes, we probably would see each other again, seeing as how Saturday was my regular day, my day off. And then he asked me where I worked.

That made him laugh again. "Really," he said. "What a coincidence" and he told me about how his grandfather or someone had had something to do with installing the machinery of the lifts.

"Well, small world," he said, with his odd smile that was always a question. "You should come round to the house, since we're already, as it were, connected – and even almost neighbours in a way. I'm just down in Brooke Street, you see. No, really, you must. Come on Christmas Eve, we always have drinks then. Do come. I'd – "

I always thought Mr Clive was actually trying to tell you something else, not saying what he was actually saying.

"Do come, I'd like to – I'd like you to. Brooke Street. Number eighteen."

There was never any chance of me saying no; he was already gone, off down the street. He was always in a hurry, Mr Clive, that's how I always think of him.

·····

So that was why the first time that I saw Brooke Street, it was on Christmas Eve, in the snow.

It's Midnight now. Happy Christmas My Darling. Sweet Dreams.

··············

Still can't sleep, one o'clock, and I have been standing by the window darling and looking out. The snow is settling so I suppose it really is Christmas now. I could unwrap my present if I wanted to. Of course if there was someone else here then I expect he'd say to me *No, you can't, not yet, you've got to wait until the morning. Come back to bed. Come back to bed now, it's cold.*

March 13th. Dinner with Clive Vivian (Brooke Street). Had only ever met Vivian the once – at the opening of Cocky's Pavilion show – but he would insist on treating one as his oldest and dearest. On my right at table a boy who solemnly informed me that he worked at Selfridges – but in such a shame-faced way that for one delicious moment I entertained the fantasy that this was merely an alibi and that he was one of the other guest's rent. It was that sort of party. Once it became clear that he was telling me the unvarnished truth we proceeded to have an entirely fascinating conversation about what one can obtain on credit these days. Almost everything, it seems.

No one else I knew, except for Messel, who I rather imagine was there because word was going round at the Pavilion that Clive had expressed interest in putting some of his supposedly sizeable inheritance into the planned all-negro *Dover Street to Dixie* which Oliver is currently working on. I should say from his choice of staff that our Mr Clive was more interested in the blond than the dusky.

The house quite fantastically ugly, the very last word in 1886 I should imagine and apparently kept as a museum piece ever since. Sort of Godwin Chelsea heavily revarnished and over-upholstered at the Chicago World Fair and then shipped direct to Mayfair to impress the new neighbours. All by the book; glassware by Liberty's and Morris curtains over the servant's door. On the way up the stairs I had a sudden disheartening sense of how stupid it is ever to believe that one is being modern, but then felt how desperately important it is to be part of sweeping all this away and letting some light in. Or at least getting away from it all. Promised myself that when I got home I would listen to Florence Mills and The Blackbirds, which I did.

Ridiculous food which I suppose was meant to be whimsical but was in fact merely indigestible. Rather good Venetian glass plates. No one seemed to really know anyone else and so of course everyone talked too much. A ridiculous story from Charles Henry Ford about Sassoon (Sir Phillip) – and a marvellous one from Oliver about Lady Londonderry attempting to wear the Stewart, Vane and Tempest jewels simultaneously and practically falling down the stairs of Lansdowne House under the sheer weight of her emeralds. Meanwhile, one hired-in waiter having to serve the entire meal single-handed so far as I could see (and making the most terrible job of it). The most marvellous hair. Like a white-gold ring that one at first assumes is simply silver. By the time the coffee came I was desperate to leave, but Vivian was helplessly drunk and proceeded to launch into a convoluted anecdote about a suicidal neighbour and how one simply can't stand it any longer and how the poor man must have been desperate, etc. I simply cannot bear that sort of thing in public. It was only when we got round to lurid speculation about leaps from second floor windows that I realised that he was talking about Loulou Harcourt killing himself the year before last after Edward James's mother had made the rounds with her accusations. The whole fuss was quite ridiculous since everybody knew that Harcourt would pounce on absolutely anything, one always had to lock the bathroom door. I didn't know where to look, and I could see that Oliver was obviously mortified. Since doing that marvellous white outfit for Tilly in Cocky's show he has got to know James rather well I think, and so must be acquainted with all the sordid details. I heard it was pills. Must ask Oliver.

Anyway, that all somehow got us round to how he, Vivian, was in an equally desperate state, something about the inheritance being spent even before he got to it, the usual Mayfair story, and how he quite knew how Harcourt must have felt (!!!!!). Then he proposed a toast, stood up, fell over and practically threw us all out. A preposterous end to a preposterous evening.

On the way home in the cab I found myself thinking about

scandals. About deaths, actually, I suppose. Apparently Vivian's mother had something of a *culte* of Wilde; and I remembered going down to Florence with Nancy after the Porter's ball in Venice and calling in on Norman Douglas and finding Reggie Turner there, talking about Wilde as if he had seen him only last week rather than thirty years ago.

Funny how one still can't talk about certain things, even if half the people in the room know perfectly well what is being alluded to.

One never does really talk I suppose. One didn't know all the people who were there, after all.

from *It Wasn't All Dancing: the Diaries of Hugo Rumboldt* (Robin Castle, ed., Routledge, London, 1989, ill., pp. 107–8)

Christmas Day

Nine. Nine o'clock, would you mind. Getting up late is not like me, because I have always thought that when you are on your own you have to stick to your routine more, not less. Monday morning, I would usually be up at seven o'clock. Still – still I suppose I did have a bit of a drink.

I had forgotten how the snow changes everything. You can tell that it's settled just by lying there and listening. There are no trains on the Camden Road bridge this morning of course, but it's not just that; there isn't any sound at all. Any there is, the snow takes it away, so that up here on the fifth floor there's nothing. Just that odd light that you get with snow, coming up off the street and under the curtains. And then when you look out everything is clean and empty. I like that. Clean white pavements. No marks, nothing. Even the bombsites down by Euston, all white.

I left this out on the table last night and it's not like me to leave anything out. Even if I hadn't written anything, even if all the pages were still empty, I still should have put it away.

Well I haven't read what I wrote yesterday because I think the important thing is probably to just get on. I want to write it down straight away with not even a cup of tea first, because there was a bit more last night. Just a bit more.

It starts the same each time. There's no snow; the snow's gone. Real bright sunlight. There is no one on the street, and I don't know why it is so quiet. I have walked here – from work I suppose.

What am I wearing? Not my work suit, I don't think, so it can't be a week day, it must be a weekend. It must be Saturday.

I have walked down Oxford Street. I turn left, Gilbert Street, and when I reach Brooke Street I cross over: I want to be on the dark side in order to get a better look at the outside of the house. In a moment I am going to cross over again, on to the bright side, and I am going to climb the steps and ring the bell. I know I am going to do that; but I am not doing it yet. For now, I am standing and staring at the house.

Nobody is going to come out.

The door is closed, the whole house looks closed.

The door has a metal grille, with the number eighteen in it, protecting a small window of thick glass – not that I can see any of that from here, but this isn't the first time that I've been here. You can't actually see the front door from across the street because of the way that the steps turn to the right, up under the arch. Above the door is the stone with the initials carved in it. Above that is the arch, and over the arch is the heavy-looking balustrade, cut out of stone, and it is a really beautiful dark red in this sunshine. The walls are made of a different stone, lighter, but still red; granite. Hammered, I think he said. Cut in great heavy blocks, which looks odd in a street like this one. And at the top the roof is red; red tiles. Looking down again slowly, there are the blank, square windows on the top floors, which must be the windows of the servants' rooms, though I have never been up there. Below them are the three full-length windows of the main bedroom, the library and the front parlour, with the balustrade in front of them. One of the windows is open. The left-hand one. The interior of the house is heated throughout to a constant winter temperature – fifty-five degrees – by a hot water system (everything about this house is modern) and today, for the first time this year, the sun has some real warmth to it, and so it must be hot in there, too hot for comfort; and that must be why one of the windows has been left open like that. The left-hand one.

And standing in the window, behind the balustrade, there is a young man, with hair that is almost white.

He is stretching his arms above his head and lifting his face to catch the sun; he hasn't shaved. He doesn't know that anyone is watching him.

For about three months now it has been the same every time.

Every night. And then last night, at this point, which is why I'm writing it down, at this point in the dream, just as I was looking at him, the date and the time when this is happening came to me exactly. I heard it. Heard it as a whole sentence, like in a book or on a guided tour. The roof is red. The walls are red. Everything in the house is modern, and it is two o'clock. Two o'clock on the afternoon of March the fourteenth.

I never do get to the end though. I wake up before that.

Sometimes you hear people say, "Oh, you look awful this morning; not sleeping again?", "Oh, believe me, it is awful, Miss Elton" (this is all in the lift first thing), "I had that terrible dream again last night" – but that's the odd thing; I would never say that. I would never say "terrible". You hear people say sometimes you should write your dreams down as soon as you wake up, so that you won't ever forget them. Well, with this dream I know I haven't remembered it all yet, but I know I certainly don't have to worry about ever forgetting it. I can run it over in my mind any time that I want to. Even at work, although I try not to do that. It's something I try to keep for the weekends, because it caught me out once in the lunch break, and I found I couldn't really stop it once I'd started, it was awful. Red eyes, blood everywhere, which caused some comment, and I did promise myself I wouldn't ever allow that to happen again.

I couldn't honestly say why it makes me wake up. I can't honestly remember what I feel when I see him like that. But it isn't sad at all really.

There must be more, of course. There must be more to remember or it wouldn't keep on coming back like this. Perhaps

I turn left off Oxford Street, and leave the crowds behind me. There is no one on the street, and I don't know why it should be so quiet at this time. I don't know if it's just because it is the weekend. Perhaps there is something wrong, perhaps there is some reason why there is no one but me walking down Gilbert Street. I think I can hear the sound of my own blood in my head. It is so quiet that I must be holding my breath. It is so quiet, I keep on imagining footsteps behind me. I am quite sure that someone is going to come after me shouting, I'll hear the footsteps and the shouting, *oi, oi you*, someone is going to grab my arm and ask me what the hell am I doing. Ask me what the hell am I thinking. Those streets on the south side of Oxford Street are like that. All the steps lead straight up to the front door (except for number eighteen), all the steps are washed and all the doors painted and all the bells polished, but all the business goes in through the back door, out of sight; you never expect to see anyone much on the street, except for people getting out of taxis. So of course someone like me shouldn't be there, even if I am wearing my best suit. The people who live behind those doors don't want anyone they aren't expecting ringing their bell. And especially not on a Sunday. So I just tell myself it's all right, it's Sunday, people go away for the weekend, that's why there is no one on the street. The people who live here all have places in the country.

So it was a Sunday, not a Saturday at all. And come to think of it, I know that the things I want to say aren't the kind of things that you should say out loud on the doorstep on a Sunday afternoon, and that is why I am holding my breath; to stop myself from saying them. I said I was scared that someone was going to start shouting in the street. Well that was me. It was me who was going to start shouting.

I have walked down Gilbert Street, I've crossed over and I have turned right, and now I am standing on the dark side of Brooke Street, underneath the lamppost, opposite number eighteen. I am just about to cross over and climb the steps and ring the bell. I know I am going to do that. But first I want to stop for a bit and start breathing again. I want to take a good look at the outside of the house. I want to stare at it. At its face.

I've remembered a new bit here; I am thinking that this is the first time that I have ever been here uninvited. All the other times, it was arranged. But this time is the only time that he doesn't know that I am going to turn up.

There up over the door is the carving with the initials (putting your name up over the door so that everyone would know; I would never want to put my name up over my door). The door is closed. The whole house looks closed; no one is going to come out and speak to me unless I cross and ring the bell. So I'll ring the bell and I'll stand there looking at the metal grille with the number eighteen in it and the sheet of coloured glass, thinking how it makes the light inside the hall golden when they close the door behind you. About how even the light in there is different, because everything is different, the light, the temperature, the sounds, or rather lack of them. Talk about a different world.

That's what I'll be thinking as I am waiting for the door to open.

But then later, when I do climb the steps, and I do ring the bell, and I wait, I discover that the door which I was so sure was closed is open. It opens when I touch it. How can it swing so easily when it is so thick and heavy?

But I can't cross the street yet, none of that can happen yet. First I have to stand on the pavement on the dark side of Brooke Street and look up at the front of number eighteen.

I have got to get this all in the right order, otherwise it won't make any sense. That's our Mr Page for you. Monday to Friday, and all in the right order.

Before, it was always night; I'm sure it's important that this is the first time that I have ever seen this house by daylight. The whole of the front of it is in sunshine, and it is that particular kind of sharp, London, spring sunshine that makes everything clear. You can see every single detail of the coloured stone and glass, and you can see just how beautiful and grand it is. This is exactly how it was meant to look when they built it. Every detail; the red roof-tiles, the great red stones, the three full-length windows of the main bedroom, the library and the front parlour. And there is the left-hand one, the one which has been left open. And there, standing in the window, behind the balustrade, is the young man, very beautiful.

He has stepped right out of the window now, out on to the ledge behind the balustrade, right into the sun. I can see all of him. His arms are up over his head and he is lifting up his face to catch as much of this sunlight as he can. He hasn't shaved. His hair is almost white, his eyes are closed, and he doesn't know that anyone is watching him.

He is naked.

I don't know how long I go on looking at him for. It is certainly one of those moments that go on for a very long time. I know that I don't look either to the left or to the right to see if anyone is coming down the street, I just keep on looking at him. I am not at all surprised to see him; isn't that odd? He is so very beautiful – nineteen, or twenty – and his white skin and his white hair against that red stone are so beautiful in that particular light, and I can see them so clearly that nothing else matters, and I am not at all surprised, or alarmed, or shocked. I am just looking at him, and I am so happy looking at him in the sunlight that I don't feel any of the things that I would expect Mr Page to feel in this situation. "Not frightened." That's probably how I would describe it. I am not looking round to see if anyone else is coming and I am not frightened.

How can he do that to me? Me of all people. Mr Page.

Perhaps he has come out into the window to feel the warmth of the sun. I am sure that it's warm, this Sunday, because I am not wearing my coat, you see; and I can remember wearing my coat all the time in those dark weeks, I mean I remember the whole business being full of scenes with me walking down the dark streets and round the squares of Mayfair seeing my breath catch in the light of the lamps, always walking fast, keeping moving because of the cold that year – London was all gloves and scarves and icy pavements and bruises, everyone was always wrapped up. Whenever I stood in the hall of number eighteen there was always the business of the taking of coats, brushing the snow off (and me thinking, *surely he shouldn't be doing this himself? Surely there should be someone to take my coat?*). Here on the dark side of the street I can still feel that cold somewhere underneath the warmth of the afternoon; this sunshine is not going to be enough to keep the frost away later. It will freeze again tonight, you can be sure of that. So perhaps that's it; he hasn't come out to warm himself, that was wrong, he's come out to feel that bite in the air, to get out of those over-heated rooms for a moment and to feel some air on his face and under his arms. The interior of the house is heated to a constant winter temperature of fifty-five degrees, you see, it's a hot water system, admirable for the time when it was put in.

I can hear a voice telling me these things, that's how I know these things. Listing all the things in the house as I'm shown round, making it more like a house you should visit than one somebody might live in. Listing all the things you can see, then telling me all about the things you're not supposed to see as well, the hidden corridors, the silver-plated fittings throughout. Every single thing in the house was chosen. Everything in the house is modern. And because I can hear the voice telling me all about it, giving me the guided tour, the young man with his arms raised and his eyes closed seems part of it. He looks like part of the whole arrangement. I mean that when you look at him like that you feel that you were meant to look at him, meant to admire him, allowed to look at him for as long as you want to. And I can see it all now, see him so exactly that I am sure that this must be exactly what I did see, I can't be just dreaming this, not his arms up over his head like that and his white hair and his face raised to catch the sun like that. Not the fact that I can see all of him.

And I can even remember the exact time and the exact date that I saw it. I looked down; that's it. I looked down and I looked at my watch. The roof is red, the stones are red – granite, I think he told me; the young man is naked, everything in the house is modern, and it is two o'clock on the early afternoon of March the fourteenth. Two o'clock on the early afternoon of March the fourteenth. 1924.

Now he's gone.

And now I'm crossing Brooke Street and I'm climbing, I'm going up the steps to the door. The door is open

and that's all. That's all there is. That really is as far as I get. Tea now. It doesn't really matter that it's Christmas morning. Doesn't matter to me. It's a day to myself, that's all.

··············

Sometimes when I'm reading History I stop and I wonder if I am being lied to. If it tells you that something happened on a particular date, say that something happened at two o'clock on the afternoon of March the fourteenth, then you want to know if that is true or not.

Obviously there is no one that you can actually ask, because it's all in the past. I do sometimes wonder with these books how you're supposed to know if they have got something right or not. And there isn't any *almost right*, is there, because either something is true, or it isn't. Either it did happen exactly like that or it didn't, and if there are any mistakes, well then, they shouldn't be allowed to get away with it, is what I think. If there is a mistake in a timetable then you miss your train. And if something is printed wrong in a first-aid manual then I don't really want to hear any excuses, I just want them to have made sure they got it right in the first place. It's the same at work; I can hardly tell a customer that I have got their bill *almost* right, can I? They wouldn't want to hear any apologies on that score and quite right too. They wouldn't want to hear any apologies because if you're too late, or if the knife slips, or if you find out when you get to the counter that you haven't got the right money and you can't afford to buy the tickets, then the consequences can be just terrible. Or if you don't get there on time. Or if you can't get them to wake up. Can't wake them up in time. If you're late.

If in a book it said, "Two or three o'clock in the afternoon", for instance, well that wouldn't do at all. You don't start work at "eight or nine o'clock in the morning", do you; you have to be there exactly five minutes before the doors open, Monday to Friday. It makes a difference. Three o'clock is a whole hour later than two, and it might be an hour too late. An hour can be a long time. You can get very worried in an hour. If you arrange for someone to arrive at a certain time and then they aren't there, then of course you worry.

I think it ought to be the same when you are remembering things. You ought to work out exactly when things happened.

And so I have, and I'm quite sure that it was two o'clock. At two o'clock the pavement on the south side of Brooke Street would have been in shadow and the fronts of the houses on the other side would have been in full sunshine, but it wouldn't have been like that an hour later, not at that time of year. And by five o'clock the sunlight wouldn't have been that sharp, and it would have been too cold – too cold for him to be naked. And frankly if the person who is telling you the story can't be trusted to tell you what time it was exactly, what day and what year, well then – well then you can't believe a word he says.

Mind you, having said that, it's not easy. I'm not making my life any easier. It's not as if I can go to the library, or as if there's a diary I can look all the details up in. As I said, I never kept a diary. We were all very young in 1924 and at the time it was all too exciting, being twenty, and then twenty-one, the last thing you had time for was writing things down. Everything's beginning, when you're twenty, and at that age it never occurs to you that you are going to need to ever remember anything, does it? I mean you never think that you are going to have to ever deliberately look back over something and work it out.

They were hardly the sorts of things that I could have written down anyway. Certainly not people's names, and addresses, which is the sort of detail that I need. I never kept anybody's address in those days, not in writing – and I still don't, actually. Habit I suppose. You didn't have to, anyway; in those days if you got as far as somebody actually telling you their address, well you weren't likely to forget it, were you, you were that excited. And even if I had kept any of them, I could hardly write now and say *hello, I don't know if you remember me, but we once met in the sixth row of the stalls at the Pavilion thirty-two years ago. Or perhaps it was during the first interval. And do you know, I can't even remember the title of that show now (and who was it who wrote that song, I'm sure you know the one I mean, the one she did in the white dress?) – but could you please write back anyway at the above, giving full particulars – full names, addresses, and so on – and who were the other six guests at that dinner party exactly?*

yours, etc.

P.S. I REMEMBER YOU

I don't think so, Officer.

There are one or two people from that time who I still see quite regularly, actually, at Jermyn Street; but that's only to say hello, not to really talk to. And of course it being so busy on a Saturday afternoon these days you don't know who everyone is and you don't know what they might think. Even if you did wait until the changing room was nearly empty and then said to one of the regulars, one of the old boys, excuse me, but could you give me your telephone number, I have to talk to you – well, that's hardly going to make people very forthcoming in the present climate, is it? Not with the headlines as they have been recently, *Actor Arrested, Solicitor Found Dead*, and so on. Those two male nurses. And then that merchant navy boy who had to give evidence. And then that university man from Manchester.

"Film Star Thrown Out".

I can just see it, going up to someone and saying *look, you must remember, so why don't you tell me, you see I need to know if there was anything, I mean if you noticed anything at the time that might explain* – well, everyone's keeping their heads down at the moment and quite right too. No raised voices. No carrying on at the moment like there is sometimes. Soliciting Male Persons for Immoral Purposes. "These Evil Men."

I certainly wouldn't give anyone my number.

What if you were out at the shops when they phoned, and the phone is in the hallway downstairs, like it so often seems to be in films where the police get involved? Because then the character lady downstairs, the Mrs Welch type (they're always the ones who answer the phone), she might just happen to let that crucial piece of information slip, *Oh yes, Officer*, she'll say, *there was a call from a young gentleman one evening last week – personal he said it was – well I didn't think anything of it at the time, being as how we never had a speck of trouble before this, always kept himself very much to himself Officer* – well it would be a bit difficult explaining to the police why your number had been found on a piece of paper in his flat wouldn't it?

I suppose I could try and check some of the details in the Public Library, though I can't imagine which shelf they'd put that sort of a book on. And the newspapers for those weeks wouldn't be any help either because it's not as if there was any scandal in this particular case. No *Man Under Train at Marble Arch* in this particular case. When I heard about that one I thought why have there been so many recently, why is that, and I remember thinking how everybody would be reading about it on the number twenty-nine in the morning, Mrs Welch downstairs would be getting all the details in her *Daily Mail*, and then in the lift at work I heard Haberdashery saying to Cosmetics in her best stage whisper, "I see it's all in the papers." And at the time I nearly turned and said to her, "Not all, Miss Elton. It's not *all* in the papers." And now I think, never mind *not all*, hardly anything at all. Hardly anything at all gets into the papers. Hardly anything at all that would be useful if you actually wanted to know what happened. And so here we are thirty-three years later and no one could possibly know.

After all, I was the only one who saw it.

··············

The invitation to go back a second time came in the staff post; *Mr Page, Banking, Selfridges*. It came on the twenty-seventh or the twenty-eighth, so it was a sort of New Year's invitation, I suppose. I don't think anyone in the Department noticed that the letter was unusual at all – certainly nobody asked me who it was from – but I saw straight away what lovely quality stationery it was. I couldn't think of anyone who would have notepaper like that – and it never crossed my mind that it would be from him, because I just assumed that he would never want to see me again after – well after the embarrassment I must have caused with my first visit. I thought that if we did ever bump into each other again he would probably avoid me or more likely have just forgotten me.

But he had remembered me. And remembered all about me. Because when I opened the envelope, there it was, in lovely big strong handwriting on that beautiful thick cream paper; an invitation to come round for tea at Brooke Street at a quarter to five on the next Saturday afternoon. He had remembered not only my name and where I worked, but also what I did on my day off, and where, and at what time; because you see a quarter to five was exactly the right time. Exactly the right time for me to come out of the London and Provincial at half-past four, as I'd told him I always did, and then to walk to Brooke Street. Along Piccadilly, crossing over at Dover Street station, then up under those great dark trees that came over the wall of the garden of Lansdowne House in those days, up into Mayfair.

I never considered not going. That would have been rude. Anyway, I thought

I suppose I thought that for some reason he wanted to be my friend. I thought he was like me; the same sort of age, the same height. The same sort of – the same sort of a situation.

I took especial care with my hair and my tie in the changing room at Jermyn Street that Saturday, and set out promptly at half-past four.

I nearly wrote *as instructed*.

As I say, I took especial care with my hair and with my tie, and when I got to number eighteen and rang the bell I was glad I did, because it was Mr Clive himself who met me at the door, and with a cigarette in his hand, I remember.

"Ah. Mr Page. Do come in."

He took my coat himself, but he didn't hang it up. He just threw it over one of the hall chairs, and walked straight up the stairs ahead of me. He wasn't being rude or anything; that was just Mr Clive's style.

It was hot, like before, and just like before there was no fire. There were no flowers in any of the vases, and no sounds in the house at all – if someone else described the house to me, now, then I think I'd imagine it like one of those costume-drama stories where the mysterious young Lord lives all alone with his dwindling fortune and his terrible thoughts, all very romantic and much discussed down in the village. As it was I remember thinking I wonder why he keeps the place so dark – and I wonder who keeps the stair-rods shining like this? *The vases, the tiles, all that marble, he can't possibly keep it all polished and dusted like this on his own.*

When he opened the door into the front room my question was answered.

He couldn't have done it on his own, and he clearly didn't have to. Laid out on a great big polished table was a tea like I'd never seen; china and linen and silver and glass and enough food for – well, for a family, or for a *salon*, I think that's what you call it; a five-tier silver cake-stand, and the teapot, spoons, knives, basins, cream-jug and sugar tongs all in silver too. Plates for the bread-and-butter and the iced fancies, napkins with lace, clementines, all sorts of things. Black and yellow figs in a little pyramid, each one with a paper frill. A cut-glass pot of honey, and one of some clear, dark jam that was almost black in the lamplight. The jam was stuck with a flat spoon that you could see shining through it, like a small silver spade. Or a knife. There were plenty of cups and plates; but no other guests.

I can't say that the sight of all that made me feel any more relaxed or welcome – it certainly wasn't what I had been expecting from the note, which had just said *do come round for a cup of tea,* or words to that effect (I thought that a cup of tea meant just a cup of tea). But in a way I was relieved, because at least I knew that the people who had prepared all this and laid it out on that lovely starched tablecloth had to be still in the house somewhere, waiting in case Mr Clive rang for more hot water or whatever. I don't know why I felt that was a comfort, or a relief – I mean I don't know what I thought was going to happen. What might have happened if the house had been as empty as it sounded. Empty and hot and silent. All the curtains drawn tight on a cold January evening.

Nobody knew I was there, you see.

Why was it that Mr Clive made me think things like that?

I was very jealous of him, even then. I wanted all that; all the things he had set out on his tea-table. Lovely things; quality.

I have spent thirty years wanting what he had. Thirty years assuming I would never have it – oh no, for thirty years it never even occurred to me that I could ever, ever have what he had. But if you had asked me that afternoon what I felt about him, then what I would have said was that I was grateful. Grateful that he'd invited me, grateful to see the inside of the house. Quite happy to be sitting there in the lamp-light, wondering if something awful and exciting might be about to happen, wondering what it must be like to actually live like this, to have all this space to yourself, to have such lovely things around you all the time, to have linen like that, to be able to break a plate and not worry about it, or to drop a cup, to be able to drop a note round on someone like me and they'd just come. I remember the cups being so thin that you could see the light coming through them.

I watched him while he poured the tea. You could see that he was quite used to all this finery (a bit like one of our girls in Glass And China); he reached for things without the slightest hesitation. He didn't even put his cigarette out. And he wasn't putting on any kind of a special display, you could see that. These things hadn't been got out specially, they weren't for best. That was how they always did things, in this house.

No wonder that afterwards I used to try and imagine what the rest of the routine was like, what he did when there was no one else in the room. The thing was you see not just that I'd never seen the inside of a house like that; I'd never seen a man living on his own before. Never. I'd only been in London a year, remember.

He poured my tea, handed me a plate, and then started talking – very much the proper hostess. When he talked, Mr Clive had that rather strained way of speaking that people often have when they have been alone in the house all day. As if he was always explaining something, even though I never asked him to explain anything.

This is the voice, telling me exactly what happened, and when, and why. I must try and get it right:

"I rather think I owe you an apology," he began. "It was all so very last minute, you see, Page. I wasn't going to bother, not this year, but then I thought, well, this is the first Christmas that I've actually been in residence since coming down, and we did always use to have people round on the Christmas Eve, so I suppose – well, after all, it is up to me now. And – "

There's a pause here while he pours himself a cup of tea. He's sitting very straight-backed with the tea in one hand and his cigarette in the other, like one of those Edgar Wallace country house ladies who pretends that she has absolutely no idea what the Chief Inspector is talking about. And of course all the time she knows that it was the young master of the house who committed that terrible crime, and that's why she is being so calm and gracious about everything.

"And I do have to be seen to be doing *something* with the place, I suppose. And so anyway, picture the scene, Christmas Eve, all the guests, your good self included, are on their way, everything's been cleaned and the wine brought up and even the pictures have been dusted for god's sake, and I've done the whole thing properly and even got extra staff in – which, as it turned out, was the fatal error – and then literally just minutes before the doorbell starts ringing I'm told that the whole thing is impossible. Everything is in some sort of a trust you see; all extra expenditure to be cleared with the trustees and so on, that sort of thing. I mean I did know all that, of course, but all our usual people are quite happy to give credit – well obviously they are, since they know it's only a few weeks to go. But not the blasted staff agency, apparently. And they've queried it with the executors or whatever. So that the very moment that the first guest arrives, your good self, as I am later informed, there I am, half dressed, stuck upstairs in the middle of the most almighty row with the family lawyer, who is standing there on Christmas Bloody Eve, if you please, telling me that according to the provisions of the estate no extra staff can be hired until my coming of age. I ask you. Things, yes; I can have things, all the bloody things I could possibly want. But men, staff, no. Ridiculous, isn't it?

"Fruitcake?"

I'm sure I remember him saying that. But there wasn't a cake. He said it without thinking I expect, because I suppose he always offered his guests cake; but he'd made a mistake. There wasn't one anywhere on the table. I didn't say anything of course, I just had some bread and butter.

"So I'm left with a house that is almost precisely forty years out of date and no staff to run it with except my Grandmother's. I mean, who you choose to have in your house with you, it's hardly something you want other people to decide for you, is it. More tea?"

Now I could see who he had got all this from: his Grandmother. This was her idea of a tea – that was probably even her chair. I wonder if his Grandmother smoked like that. She was obviously a very formidable person from the way he talked about her.

"Staff you can trust, Page, that's the thing – our neighbour here had the most marvellous man. Harcourt – did ever you meet him?" (I remember thinking, oh yes, I know lots of people with staff – although actually of course Mr Clive was quite right, I could have met him, because a lot of Mayfair people do shop with us. It's one of our excitements, discussing who's been spotted and what they ordered this time, whose portrait was brought in by that nice Mr Beaton to be developed in Photographic last week.) "Anyway when the money comes through I am going to insist on taking charge of the whole situation. I know finding the right men has been difficult for everybody since the war, but really. I don't mind inheriting these rooms – but not the people in them. She called me in here once so that I could watch her do it; I suppose it must have been for the cook or the housekeeper or someone, otherwise they would have just been sent round to the back door and the butler would have dealt with it all. She stood me over there in the corner and told me to watch carefully – she was always very big on the idea that one day the house would be mine, you see.

'Clive,' she said" – he did this bit in an American voice –

" 'Clive, references may give some idea of character, face and dress may speak volumes, but one must still ask the right questions.' "

Here he gave one of his odd laughs to himself. He was very good at doing her, I must say. You could just see her, sitting there.

"And personally I couldn't agree with Grandma more. After all, they are going to be living in one's house, one can't be too careful. One boy who I've got here now for instance, who turned up on Christmas Eve itself – I mean literally about an hour before the guests were due – the whole place was in an absolute uproar, I didn't have the slightest idea who he was, and then the very first time I set eyes on him he – "

Mr Clive paused just very slightly here, and put his cup down. And then picked it up again. I think I remember his hand shaking slightly. And then he seized the silver cream jug and brandished it as if it were a piece of evidence –

" – the very first time I set eyes on him he was polishing the Georgian silver with absolutely nobody watching him – I mean one piece, one piece of a service like this would be a year's wages for a boy like that. Well, I say 'boy', he's nineteen. And I had no idea at all where he had come from, he was just an agency recommendation.

"I suppose you could say that he was all they had left on Christmas Eve."

He got up from the table here and went to the window and lifted one of the curtains for a moment – to see if it had started snowing again, I suppose. The bad weather lasted well after Christmas that year.

Except that now when I remember him doing that it looks as though he is checking to make sure that there is no one outside the house watching it, no one standing on the other side of Brooke Street under the lamppost and keeping an eye on things.

I am trying very hard to write it all down exactly. The exact way he put things, and the sound of his voice, the way he talked and talked and talked as if he had had no one to talk to all day, but never said – well never said for instance exactly who else was in the house with him. And never got round to telling me why he hadn't come down to talk to me himself on Christmas Eve. And never said who the other guests were to have been; if they were friends or if they were people he had just met in the street, like me. And he never told me why the butler or whoever it was who had taken my coat on that occasion wasn't there any more.

"You know, Page, after all those years of being told that everything was to be kept exactly as it was, I do sometimes have the distinct impression that it's the house that is running me, rather than vice versa. Perhaps I just need to get myself a manual – do you think they might have something suitable in one of your many departments? 'The Modern Home', 'The House Proper', something like that. 'The House Beautiful' was what my Grandmother called it. 'Everything In This House Is Modern'; that was always the last line of the guided tour, standing there at the top of the stairs and declaring to some unfortunate guest, 'Yes, sir, everything in this house is modern.' Which must have been all rather marvellous before I was born but is hardly convincing in this year of grace 1923. I sometimes long to go mad and pay someone to paint the whole thing white. Or at least to make some sort of a statement in the hallway, you know, something to indicate that this is now a 'bachelor establishment', as they say. Boxers, possibly. Boxing prints. Or something in uniform. What do you think? Did you notice, by the way, that it's already got my initials up over the front door? 'Carved in Stone', as they say. Rather prophetic don't you think?

"Anyway apparently there's absolutely no question of my selling it.

"Look Page I'm sorry for going on like this but it is all rather at the front of my mind at present. After Christmas comes the New Year and all that. It's only eleven weeks, and then, hey presto, twenty-one today and I can run the place how I like. Some sort of celebration is in order I think. You must come – March the thirteenth. When's yours?"

Fortunately I had just put my teacup down or I think I would have dropped it. As it was I blushed horribly (blood everywhere) and just told him. Blurted it out. Obviously it was a bit embarrassing, because there he was talking about his twenty-first being a major social event, and the fact that mine was going to be on the same day made the difference between us all the more obvious somehow. Someone like me, who worked in a shop, even if it was the biggest shop in London, was hardly going to start talking about coming into estates and running things how he really wanted to. My idea of a celebration was very different to his.

Mr Clive looked down at the napkin he was holding and slowly smoothed it out in his lap, and folded it up, and held it, staring at it; then he looked straight at me in that odd way he had, and said, very quietly, "Well, then I suppose you know just what it's like, Mr Page. Being twenty, I mean, and waiting to be twenty-one. Wanting a life of one's own."

I surprised myself by saying that yes, I did know; but he wasn't listening to me. His eyes had wandered to the other door in the room, the one we hadn't come in through.

"A life," he said, speaking very quietly all of a sudden, as if he really was talking to himself now; "A life of one's own. That's the thing. Then everything in this house *will* be modern."

Then he grinned at me, gave his little laugh to himself, as if I was somehow supposed to know what he meant, and he was off again, as if that last bit of the conversation had never happened.

"Well, enough explanations," he said. "I expect you'd like to see round the house now. Quite remarkable, of its kind, or so I'm told."

I thought, well if he's explained anything, then I've obviously missed it, but there was no time to ask, because he was already out of the front parlour and on to the first floor landing, explaining as he went, and we were off on the guided tour.

Nearly an hour, it took – you could get round this flat in ten minutes, I should think – and in that hour he told me literally everything, he told me the story of every single picture and tile and vase. He showed me the library, the front parlour, the dining-room, the study, the hall with its electric lilies, the African marble fireplace, the Japanese vase, *Staff bedrooms – hardly of any interest to you – family bedrooms – mine's up there – bathrooms – silver fittings throughout which always seems to have been a particular point of family pride, for some reason. What else can I tell you, Mr Page? Heating direct from the furnace room to a constant winter temperature of fifty-five degrees, as you will no doubt have noticed, double ceilings to eliminate the carrying of any sound from one part of the house to another, and, of course, my grandfather's Staff Corridors, giving such remarkably convenient and sudden access to all the rooms in which service is required* – now we were standing back where we had started, on the first-floor landing, with the six mahogany doors. On the wall in between two of the doors there was a beautiful curtain, all embroidered with leaves and thorns (like the forest just before the interval in *The Sleeping Beauty*). Mr Clive was standing just by it; as he did the bit about "all rooms in which service is required" he drew back the curtain and threw open the door – the seventh door – which was hidden behind it. It was exactly like the trick when the magician promises you that the cabinet is going to be empty, and you know that it can't possibly be, and then it is. The corridor behind the door wasn't like any other part of the house that he had showed me. After all the luxury and linen and panelling and the glass and the polish and the golden light, everything strange and expensive and made to last you a lifetime, this was something that I recognised: a long bare corridor, white-tiled, lit by a long row of unshaded bulbs. If you had never seen anything like it before, then I suppose you would have said it looked like a butcher's shop, or perhaps like the steam room at the London and Provincial must look when the boiler fails – but of course I thought it looked just like the corridors at work. Mr Clive explained to me how every room in the house had a hidden door, so that visitors need never see the staff, but I already knew all about that – the world that the customers never see. All the running and ordering and carrying that they never see. All so that they can imagine that when they ask for something, it's there as if by magic. That's the whole point. As Mr Clive said, "What you don't want people to see, they don't see"; and I said, "Yes, I know" again, which made him look at me, again.

He was right, of course; three times I was there and I never did know exactly who else was in the house, or where.

Before we left the landing he also told me all about the snow scene and the other pictures, *some of my Grandfather's souvenirs, Antwerp, Bruges, Brussels, Paris. Such travels.* And all about the shelf of vases. As he pointed to each of them in turn up there on their high shelf his voice tightened a bit, and just for a moment I got the distinct impression that what he actually wanted to do was to reach up and run his hand slowly, deliberately along the shelf so that, as he described each vase in turn, it would fall, each one shattering with that odd, light noise that an electric light bulb makes if you drop it, so that there'd be nothing left except gold glass splinters on the marble and he'd never have to describe them to anyone ever again.

And then he said, quite suddenly, as if he was suddenly very tired of the whole thing, "Well, that concludes the tour."

All the time he was showing me round I was listening very carefully. I couldn't help thinking, *yes, lovely, it's all lovely, but it's not yours, is it – and not just because we're both still only twenty. They weren't your travels, and they aren't your things, and it isn't even your name up over the door –* Charles B. Vail, that was the grandfather, he told me all about him and his corridors and his lifts; and Mr Clive's real name was Clive B. Vivian – C. B. V. It was just a coincidence. A coincidence carved in stone, what a funny idea. You got to the end of the tour, you got to the end of the list, of the whole inventory, and when you got to the bottom of it you found out that he hadn't even signed his real name.

··············

I have just read this last bit through again and I think I have done quite a good job of getting down the way he talked and the impression that he made on me, but what I can't remember is why I never asked him the obvious question; why did he want to have me in his house, much less tell me every single thing there was to know about it? I have been in situations where people have talked and talked and talked because they are nervous, nervous of getting round to it, nervous of spitting it out – but not Mr Clive, surely. Even the suggestion about the boxing pictures in the hall, that was some sort of a joke, not a proper explanation, not even a hint. We may have met on Jermyn Street, but not in that way. And if what he actually wanted was just to talk, to have somebody to talk to, if there was something that he needed to talk about that he couldn't talk about on the street, then why had he invited me on Christmas Eve, when he had planned to have a house full of people? And more to the point, if that was the case, then why, now that there were just the two of us, couldn't he come out and say it? I thought that he might be going to take me back into the parlour and that we'd have more tea and he would finally come out with it and tell me why I was there; but no, that really was the end of the tour up there on the landing. He took me down the stairs, showed me out himself, thanked me for coming, said that we must meet again, and then, right there on the doorstep, he asked me, in a very deliberately casual sort of way, if I would be going to the baths again. I said that I would, and he said that he still hadn't got those cufflinks, so perhaps we would see each other again there.

People always say you can tell, but nowadays I look back and I think perhaps it's not true; you can't always tell. With someone like Mr Clive you can't tell what they want from you. What they want you for. All I knew was that it was something to do with the fact that we looked the same. That was the only way I could explain it to myself because it was the only thing I could think of that we had in common. The fact that when the tour was over and we were standing on the doorstep of number eighteen and we shook hands, our eyes were exactly level again.

And now he knew something else about me. My birthday, I mean.

Sometimes I wish I could invite him back here and sit him down and tell him things and ask him things, tell him all about these thirty years. Turn the tables on him. I'd have the gas on full, to remind him of the heat, and of course it would be silent, what with the snow, just like it always was in Brooke Street. I'd like to see Mr Clive's face when he walked in here and saw how I've got my walls done, and how it's me who's got his grandfather's precious snow scene to stare at now. And I wouldn't do it like he did, I wouldn't give him the guided tour and explain everything to him; I'd just let him work it out for himself. Work out why I've got it like this, what made me do that.

What he'd done to me.

Would we still look like each other, I wonder? I often ask myself that first thing in the morning, when I'm in the lift at work. They're mirrored, you see. There is Mr Page, Banking, and there face to face with him in the gold glass mirror is his double, the other Mr Page – sometimes I think I can even see him smiling. Actually I'm surprised that no one ever complains about the decoration in the lifts. All that black and gold glass and then over the doors all the twelve signs of the Zodiac done in gilded bronze. It's not what you expect first thing in the morning on respectable premises. Each sign has a naked man in it – with his back turned, or course, or with a bit of towelling, so that it's all very classical. A bit like Myrna Loy's bathroom in *The Barbarian*. Taurus, with his bull and his rope and his lovely back-muscles, Aquarius stripped off completely and looking like something out of that article on "Promising Newcomers" in last month's *Films and Filming*; I'm sure Miss Loy would approve. And the Gemini, the Gemini of course are Mr Clive and me, eye to eye again after all these years. All golden, and all shining, what with the heat. One of them has got the other by the shoulders, and you can't tell if he is giving in or still struggling. They are supposed to be wrest-ling, of course, being Greek – but it hardly looks as if they are fighting to me. Not the way they are staring into each other's eyes like that.

I suppose that in 1923, when Mr Clive was giving me the guided tour of Brooke Street, those golden gates would still have been almost new. I wonder if they kept the machinery that Mr Clive's grandfather had installed? The latest thing. We still had the uniformed lift girls then, with their white skirts and hats, which would look terribly old-fashioned now – but back then it was all the rage, the whole effect was very modern, as Mr Clive might have said. They always used to make me think of *Our Miss Gibbs* or *The Girl in the Taxi*, one of those old shows where the girl marries the toff and gets everything she ever wanted and everybody in the upper circle cheers. You don't get shows like that now. People say they were ridiculous, but in fact of course it really did use to happen. That was why all the girls were so keen on those uniforms; men used to come and ride up and down in the lifts just to see them, and if it was a gentleman killing time in the West End shopping for some cufflinks or something then you should have seen our girls go to work on him, *"Gentleman's Outfitting? – certainly Sir, First Floor, Going Up"*. And it used to work; a lot of them married customers, and it was always a cause for general celebration. They used to announce it in the store magazine and then it would be *Oh Miss Elton, did you hear, good for her etc. etc.* all over the Department, and everyone was glad of course, because it was a sort of a revenge on all the customers when one of the lift girls struck lucky like that. You had to be very good-looking for that job.

After 1946, after they'd unbricked the windows on Oxford Street and all the lights were on again, they had the servicemen who couldn't get jobs doing it. Funny, I never heard of one of them getting married, if you see what I mean. Perhaps they should have put them in uniform, I'm sure that would have done the trick with some of our West End customers. Some of our Gentlemen.

Every weekday morning for all these years I've been shut up in there. Going up, listening to Cosmetics and Haberdashery and catching sight of that other Mr Page in the glass, and nobody has ever known what I'm really thinking. And first thing in the morning, too. Sometimes I do wonder where that fine old machinery might be taking us. Sometimes I think that one morning the golden gates will slide open and we'll all be somewhere that the other passengers won't even begin to recognise. And there will be Mr Clive, opening his arms to greet me, taking me by the shoulders, looking me in the eye, asking me how it's been, how it's been all these years.

More tea, and then I should get dressed really. Get some clothes on. And turn that gas down.

············

It should be something you do in the other room, with the lamps on, really, not right here on the dining table. Should be something you do after it's got dark. I suppose that's why Mr Clive never had the lights on in the hall, why even when the first sun came it was still dark in there. Dark and quiet and hot.

Out here it's still bright. Sunlight.

I'm standing in Brooke Street, I'm looking up at the front of the house, and I can see everything, every single detail, exactly as it always is, with the red roof and the three tall windows. And the left-hand one of them is open, and there he is. (Now I think of it, that must be another reason why he has his arms up over his head like that. It's because he's been kept out of the light for so long. Keep a bird shut up under a blanket like that and he's bound to want to stretch his wings when he feels the first real sunshine of spring.) And I am looking up at him standing there in the window, with his arms up over his head, and his hair is white and the sun is just catching his face, and I can see all of him – and there is something that was missing before. Something to do with the moment when I know exactly what time it is.

Looking at him, it always feels very calm, at first; but then, the moment after that, I panic.

Because he opens his eyes.

He opens his eyes, and he looks round over his shoulder, into the room behind him. And just before he does that, he smiles. And the smile is what makes me know what is happening, what makes me panic, because there is only one reason why a man would turn round and look over his shoulder with a smile like that. Someone has called out his name. Someone is calling to him, saying *come back to bed*. Come to bed. Come back to bed in the middle of the afternoon. And the moment that that happens, all the blood goes into my face. All of a sudden it's so hot that I can't bear it. That's always what happens to me when I panic, ever since I was a boy, and when it happens I always look down, because I'm trying to hide my face, ever since I was thirteen or fourteen which is when this blushing started. I try and hide my face, because of all the blood. I don't want anyone to see the blood. And when it happens again now I am fourteen again, and I know I shouldn't look, I shouldn't be looking; I know that this isn't something that you should be looking at. And then, you see, what I always pretend to do is to put one of my gloves on or look at my watch, to try and make it look natural that I'm hiding my face. I look at my watch, because when I was fourteen that was what I had seen them do in the cinema. The camera would catch someone at it and it would move in closer and try and show us if they'd been caught out or not, how badly they were blushing, and of course they would have to pretend that they hadn't seen anything, that they hadn't been looking really, and that's when they would do that trick of looking down at their watch.

I knew that there wasn't anyone there on the street to catch me at it, I already knew that, but I still had to pretend that I hadn't seen anything. And so that is why I looked down, and that is why I know so clearly that it is two o'clock on the early afternoon of March the fourteenth.

Then I look back up, and then it's all familiar again; he's gone in, I cross Brooke Street, the steps turn to the right, and the heavy door swings open. It's dark. It's hot, even though there's no fire. It's too dark, it's too hot; I feel very over-dressed for the occasion. I want to take something off. I want somebody to come and take my coat, because I'm still blushing, I'm too buttoned up, there's too much blood in my head, thumping. I'm walking up the stairs and because it's so quiet I can hear Mr Clive's voice telling me where everything is and what everything means and where it all came from and I'm trying not to be distracted because I know that somewhere in the house he's here. I saw him just a moment ago, he must be here, somewhere, and I've got to find him. Which room is he in? He's always just on the other side of a door. Every time you open one, he's gone. But this time I'm going to find him, I'm going to catch him, because I know he's in there somewhere. I'm going to find him. He must be up there somewhere in one of the rooms Mr Clive didn't show me. Maybe he'll be face down with his legs slightly apart and one of the pillows ready under him, and he'll look up over his shoulder at me. Stark naked in this heat I shouldn't wonder. You've got to go carefully up those stairs if you want to catch him like that, you've got to take care not to slip and fall on all that polish – just think of the noise if those vases should start to fall from their shelf. And you're wondering which of the seven doors to open, which corridor he's running down because he's guessed you're coming. If you throw back the curtain and open the door quick enough then maybe you'll catch him out – but he's not there. Start again.

There is no fire in the hall and there is no noise and there are no signs of life at all. I'm starting to climb the stairs, I'm reaching the landing with the closed doors, and now I'm at the top of the stairs, I can hear the sentence again, the sentence with the date and the time that tells me exactly when this is happening. Telling me that I mustn't ever forget this. Two o'clock on the fourteenth of March. And the voice that I'm hearing is Mr Clive's voice. Did I write that down last time? The voice that I hear saying the sentence is the voice Mr Clive used when he showed me round the house. And the other thing that I've realised is that I haven't written down his name. When Mr Clive said it I think he said it in the boy's own language, Gabrijels. But I have always thought of him as Gabriel, and so that's how I'll write it. Gabriel. Gabriel with his hair so blond it looked white.

The second invitation came by hand, and this time half the Department must have seen it, and those that didn't actually see it arrive soon heard all about it, I should think. Imagine me, Mr Page, looking up from my order book, thinking it was just going to be the next customer, and instead seeing Gabriel, in the middle of the morning, in the middle of the week, in the middle of the Department, carrying a letter in his white-gloved hand. And walking straight towards me. He didn't say anything, and I'm sure I didn't either. I just stared at him as he handed me the envelope ("Mr Page, Banking, By Hand"), bowed, turned smartly on his heel, and left.

He couldn't have caused more of a stir if he'd actually come in through the window carrying a bunch of lilies and speaking Latin like his name-sake. To go with the white gloves he was wearing a high-collared, gold-buttoned page-boy tunic, so that he looked like he'd been designed for a Christmas window. Or to be a footman in the chorus of an operetta, one of the big Drury Lane shows. Something set somewhere with a lot of blossom and soldiers and a big cathedral for the second-act finale. Except that I shouldn't think any producer with any sense would have stuck him in the chorus; with that hair and those looks you'd have had him right down at the front with a silver tray or holding the train on the coronation robes. A lovely dark red wool, the jacket was, and cut very tight. High lapels, sixteen buttons down the front, and four on each cuff. Black moleskin trousers. Dark red and gold to go with the colours of Number Eighteen I suppose – we must have looked like that bit in the panto when the messenger from the palace arrives in all his finery to deliver the invitation to the Ball, and he doesn't even deign to speak to that Cinderella, she looks so ordinary. But Gabriel wasn't being rude when he turned on his heel and left with just a stiff little half bow and without saying a word, because of course he couldn't. Couldn't speak any English at all.

Although I didn't know that then.

I stood there like a fool with the envelope in my hand trying furiously not to blush, and failing of course. And trying not to stare at Gabriel walking away from me in those perfectly cut black trousers. And all my colleagues pretending not to stare at me, standing there acting as if this was all quite normal and Mr Page always received his morning mail like this.

I kept on working as best I could and then at lunchtime I went straight to the staff toilet and locked myself in and opened the envelope.

It was that beautiful heavy cream paper again; I tried to open it without tearing it, but I couldn't. Inside was a stalls ticket for a show at the London Pavilion, and a note scrawled on his headed notepaper, just saying, "Do Come". No name or anything, no explanation. And I hadn't seen or heard from him for weeks.

Of course I went.

Sonnie Hale, Jessie Matthews (in the chorus; it must have been one of her very first shows) and Tilly Losch it was, all in the one show; *and* it was the first night. *The Latest Thing*, it was called – Mr Cochran's shows always had titles like that – and I made sure I got there good and early so that I could see everyone arriving. Everyone going in in their furs and their evening dresses, people I'd only ever heard about. It was wonderful. Mr Cochran arriving, everyone telling him how marvellous they'd heard it was – it was the one with the famous scene all done in white, and people were talking about it even before it opened. All the foyer was done up in white too, great banks of white lilies, and I got pushed up against them; I remember trying to not get the pollen on my suit, which I'd hired, and failing, and trying to brush it off without attracting attention to myself and thinking *oh god don't look at me, everyone here knows everyone, except me. I wish he would come.* Because he was late of course.

There I was with the golden pollen all down my lapels and

trying not to blush and looking at my watch every other minute – I always seem to be looking at my watch in this story, don't I, getting dressed up, worrying about getting somewhere exactly on time and then thinking perhaps I've got the wrong time or I've come to the wrong place. I was always either practising what I was going to say when he finally arrived or trying to quickly think of an answer to a question I hadn't expected. He was always catching me out. That's what I remember most – not all the bits in between, the catching the number twenty-nine every day and walking down Oxford Street – it's the waiting, the waiting for the extraordinary things to happen. Waiting for Mr Clive to turn up. Waiting until the very last minute, and then there being that awful feeling of panic when the bells went off and thinking that perhaps they wouldn't let me in without him, because if one of the ushers asked me who I was and how on earth had I got hold of that ticket, what would I say; and then more panic when I did go in, sitting in the dark with the empty seat beside me as the overture started and my face starting to burn, blood everywhere, because I thought that people would see that my dress suit was only hired and that it didn't quite fit as well as it might have and then they'd know that I couldn't possibly have paid for my own seat, not right there in the middle of the best row of the stalls on the opening night.

I don't remember much of the show itself, although there was one number that I can still see quite clearly; the curtain went up, and there was Sonnie Hale singing "Dance, Dance, Dance", and Miss Losch was with him. She was wearing a strange dress that I think must have been made of white rubber or plastic, from the way it moved; she walked slowly along a line of dancers, all grinning, all wearing shiny black suits that made them look more like dolls than people, and you could see that she couldn't dance any more, because she was too tired, there was this wonderful effect of everybody being too tired to carry on but not being able to stop. And the clever thing was that you didn't realise straight away that they were all wearing masks. They just all had these odd, slightly staring eyes, as if something awful had happened, but no one could bring themselves to say anything about it. Everyone went mad at the end of that number, it was a sensation.

Noel Coward, that's who the song was by. People say that the shows aren't the same now, and it's true that it does seem like another time now, especially with the kind of music you hear these days, but it's not, is it? Because he's still working, isn't he, Mr Coward? Two years ago, when they had one of the charity fashion shows, with all sorts of people, Petula Clark and HRH The Princess Margaret and so on, Mr Coward did the cabaret for it. Very tanned and wearing rather too much make-up I thought for something in the middle of the afternoon, but nobody said anything, at least not that I heard. I kept on wondering if he still knew the words to that song or if he might sing it. Very tired, but not able to stop, that was exactly what he looked like. I've never really cared for that sort of person but that afternoon I almost went up to him and told him how much I admired him. Almost asked him if he still remembered the words.

When Mr Clive did turn up it was right in the middle of a number, squeezing past everybody to get to his seat and whispering *Hello, hello darling* to everybody. "Hello, Page" was all he said to me; no explanations, as usual. Then in the interval he was too busy talking to absolutely everyone to talk to me, promising drinks and dinners and parties on the spur of the moment and at the top of his voice. I thought, he can't possibly know all these people. He certainly made sure that everybody knew that he was there, ordering champagne and then talking so much that he never had time to drink any, keeping me standing there holding the dripping silver bucket for him. Shouting at people that they must be sure to telephone him as the bells went for the second half.

He had money written all over him that night, our Mr Clive, money dropping off him every time he moved; there were people clustering round him like they could smell it. A perfect dress suit (well that's what a Jermyn Street tailor can do for you), champagne, sapphires (so he'd been and got those cufflinks), stalls seats, promises – that was Mr Clive on a West End night.

What else do I remember? Walking home, when everyone else had got into taxis. Feeling rather drunk and rather smart and fashionable.

There being a Mr James there, who was something to do with

the show – and the way that Mr Clive seemed to know him, but didn't seem to want to talk to him. And the way that Mr Clive would introduce people to each other as if they were his dearest friends and I could see from the way that they looked at him that they weren't at all sure. The way that he shouted at people, grabbed at people, grabbed their arms.

And his leaving before the end – of course. In the applause just before the final number he leaned over and whispered something about money to me, something about difficulties with money again. "*Don't ask, but listen, Page, you must come round to dinner one night, all right?*" He did it when the applause was quite loud; I had the distinct impression he didn't want anyone else to hear – as if it was me who was his closest friend, as if the others didn't really count.

He was always either late or early, Mr Clive. The more splendid he got, the closer he got to all that money of his, the more of a hurry he seemed to be in. As if he was late, as if it was always getting late, too late. As if he'd slept too late – or never slept enough, had stayed up half the night. That was it; as if he'd been up half the night. As if he was never quite at ease in those wonderful clothes of his.

Presumably there were lots of other nights like that during that January and cold February of 1924, lots of other nights when he went out on the town and made sure everybody could see him. This just happened to be the one that I was summoned to witness. He must have been doing all this to other people as well as to me, he must have been. I can't have been the only one, surely.

I should be getting that lunch on because you can't open your presents until after lunch, can you? Get that bird in the oven, except that there's no bird. Lay that table, except that there's just me. Open that other bottle except that you know the second one only makes you feel worse.

The Key to the House

To look upon each minute as precious and to be exchanged only for its full equivalent in Progress; to realise that Time is the only Commodity of which everyone has an equal amount; to know that every hour of each day's Service builds a happier future and to feel that the waking hours after the day's work is over are best used in agreeable companionship and in those acts and recreations that best build a happier Character; to find in the life of The House an occasion for every pleasure and for the satisfaction of that greatest search, the search for what is good and what is true.

To pursue the True Dream and Goal and to admit of no obstacle as insurmountable.

Gordon Selfridge Senior

First written for the opening of Marshall Field's State Street store in Chicago (1879) and then adapted by Selfridge for the opening of his premises in London in 1909. Reprinted in the Coronation edition of the staff magazine The House of Selfridge, *1953.*

unwrapped my present. Thank you very much Mr Page oh that's all right, Happy Christmas Mr Page. Have another drink Mr Page, well that's very kind of you I don't mind if I do Mr Page. If I had anybody here to talk to if there was anybody here that I could talk to if this was the sort of thing that you could talk about then I wouldn't be sitting here having had no proper breakfast worth speaking of just two pots of tea and two large whiskies at half-past twelve of a Christmas morning half naked in a grey silk dressing gown bloody writing it all down, would I? And as I said already no reference is intended to any actual person still living, which he is I assume though not of course in this country, and anyway I hardly knew him. Which is to say I only met him in November twenty-three and they were gone by the time the snow went although of course it did stay late that year. Hardly even a full six months so you could hardly say that I knew him and you certainly wouldn't say that I knew him well. So you see I'm really not the right person to be asking about him at all, Officer. And no reference is intended to any persons now dead. No reference at all. None whatsoever. And as for places, I am of course as you know and as I have readily admitted Officer still at the same address both as far as living and employment go (Yes, Officer, over thirty years in the same Department, it's splendid really when you think of it) and have therefore attempted to keep my own place of residence here on the fifth floor discreetly disguised or concealed, however it has been necessary in the interest of historical accuracy to make all details of bus routes and times, Departments and staffing arrangements as correct as possible, still, no offence meant to any particular parties who may have been named. I suppose you could work out the address for yourself, Officer; let's see, suitable area for someone just starting in the Department in 1923, now considerably run down I should say from the apparent low tone of the other residents e.g. Mrs Welch and the *Daily Mail* underneath, within earshot of rail traffic on the Camden Road bridge, not too far from Wellington Street Market to carry heavy shopping even when tired after work on a Friday evening, handy for the number twenty-nine bus route – oh well done, Officer, that must be you knocking at the door now. Just a moment while I unlock it. Yes Officer I am fully aware of the very serious charges that may be brought. Yes Officer I am fully aware of the very serious possible consequences of making an incorrect statement under these circumstances believe you me. Certainly Officer, let's go through my statement once more. A young man appearing naked, in the middle of the afternoon. And in W1. *Thirty-three years ago you say, sir.* But really Officer, we went through all this last night. Well all right just the once more if you insist. I was walking in a southerly direction down Gilbert Street – and then the other officer joins in, the younger one, I must say I think he's rather good-looking this one – and yes Officer I do have a particular or shall we say personal reason for finding this all so memorable. *Right sir, let's try again, shall we? The steps were red, you said, sir, and this was at number nineteen* – Oh no Officer (really I don't know why they try and catch you out on the details with that old trick, do they think people like me don't go to the pictures, do they think we don't know how it's done?) – this was at number eighteen. Number Eighteen Brooke Street West One. Yes Officer of course, of course you may read your notes back.

> "I am quite sure that I am seeing what it was that I actually saw. His body. His arms. Up over his head, with his hands resting on his white hair and his face apparently raised to catch the sun. I can remember the exact time and date that I saw this. I suppose I must have looked down and caught sight of my watch. The roof was red, the stones were red, the Young Man in question was naked, everything in the house was modern, and it was two o'clock precisely on the early afternoon of March the fourteenth. 1924."

Yes Officer that is quite correct. Yes Officer I am quite sure about the date. Yes Officer I am fully aware of the possible consequences of appearing naked, of a man appearing naked at the wrong time and in the wrong place. Even in Jermyn Street for instance you have got to watch yourself on that score. Regulations concerning the wearing of towels are strictly enforced, Mr Maguire Chief Attendant sees to that Officer. Otherwise it is quite clear what you and the other man are up to, especially in the current climate, articles in the newspapers and so on. Although in this case there was of course nothing at all in the papers, no mention of it not even on page five, despite the fact that there could have been no doubt at all what the two of them had been up to which is obviously unacceptable as you so rightly say, Officer. Even if one of the parties concerned was to later become quite famous for taking his clothes off in public, at least partially, and I say "in public", I mean of course only insofar as a film is in public. But at least it is all done in the dark, thank goodness for that Officer, even though it may be in the very heart of London's West End and it may be the middle of the afternoon and even though some members of the general public may find it quite surprising that we're all sitting there in rows watching Marines or whatever the excuse is this afternoon wearing little more than machine-oil above the waist, and invariably sweating of course with all that stunt-work – at least it is all done, as is proper, in the dark. And also I should like to point out Officer that he wasn't really that well known at the time, so that there was no element of what you might call exposure in the incident referred to. Not that I'm saying that his appearance didn't cause some raised eyebrows amongst the older clientele, but that was more to do with his appearance in only a towel and fresh from the steam room rather than us knowing his name. His picture as featured in *Films and Filming* some weeks later did of course cause some considerable comment amongst the Saturday morning regulars. In fact Officer I think we, I mean I, may well have kept that issue, I am sure I have it somewhere to hand, if you could just let me – funny isn't it Officer, going back to my statement for a moment, if that had been a film, then I would have been able to stare at him for as long as I wanted and there would have been none of this embarrassment and no need for these questions. If it had been a film then there would have been no question of anyone being able to see the expression on my face or to wonder what I was thinking, because we would all have been sitting in the dark and no one would have been able to even hazard a guess. And of course if it was all just a dream, well Officer, if it's a dream, then I can see him standing there and I can have this moment go on all afternoon, right up until the evening showing, I can't have it go on all night if I want it to. I can stand right there in the street and because it is a dream there is no one to see me doing it and I can watch him for hours and hours and no one can stop me. There is nothing anyone can do to stop me now. Not even you Officer, not even Mr Maguire Chief Attendant or Mrs Welch or The Misses Elton or the *Daily Mail*. Nothing anyone can do to change the fact that I saw what I saw.

I can stare at him for as long as I want to.

I can see him just like it was yesterday.

And of course if it was all just a dream, well then as you so rightly say that is my own private and of no possible consequence, however – oh no, Officer, I am absolutely sure about the time and the date. Two o'clock on the afternoon of – and do you know, Officer, and I am sure these details will all prove relevant to your enquiry in the end, I've often thought I really should have taken that dressing-gown when I had the chance. Then I could have dressed myself up in it and had a good stare at myself in the bathroom mirror and then I really would have been able to see how he looks these days with none of all this *I can almost remember* and *Funny isn't it after all these years* nonsense. I should have taken it because then I would have a real silk dressing-gown on this afternoon, his dressing-gown, and it would be a perfect fit, and you would have an accurate and up-to-date description – I assume you are still looking for him, Officer, even after all these years. Because as you have doubtless noticed – well you did always have such an eye for detail, Officer, and it is always these little details and half-truths that you catch us out on – what I am actually sitting here wearing is the Less Expensive, not the Jermyn Street. That tell-tale taste for luxury is always such a dead giveaway in these cases, I couldn't agree more. Taking all his clothes off in the middle of the afternoon with a glass of whisky and the gas on and his fancy gold-pleated lampshades and now pretending he's slipping into something a little more expensive, who does he think he's fooling? You can't mistake the feel of real silk against the skin, can you, Officer? Me and my drinking before lunchtime. Still at least I remembered to lock the door. Habit of a lifetime. And then of course one day, well nobody was more surprised than me, one day the door isn't locked at all, it swings open, you go up the stairs, oh sodding lunchtime, sodding Christmas, sodding Christmas bloody lunch, tea and dinnertime, sod it, there's no bird, no cranberry, not even so much as a single sodding roast potato, and me not even dressed – *not much of a Christmas for you, is it?* I don't know why I didn't get more in, I don't know who I thought it was going to help, me camping out like this, doing my *On your own again I expect this year?* routine. They do say that more people do it over the Festive Season than at any other time, and come to think of it the funny thing is even with the books you read and all the stories in the papers this year I never once thought of doing it myself, never once.

Can't write any more now darling, sorry.

You're quite right there, Officer Maguire, my sense of time can be a bit – oh no, Officer, I am absolutely sure about the time and the date. Two o'clock on the afternoon of – Yes, sir, thank you. I think we have all that down already. March the fourteenth and so on. Now, if you could just sign that for me sir? *Catch me putting my name to that sort of thing you must be bloody joking Officer.*

··············

The same, later that afternoon, as they say. Well I fell asleep. Should have known it would happen if I sat down here with the gas on. That's one of the changes I notice most; now quite often I do drop off on a Saturday afternoon.

The changes in the way your actual body works, you don't

notice them so much, not as much as you notice the new buildings or the new clothes. Because the body happens bit by bit, I
suppose. There is more hair on the small of my back now, but
apart from that when I see myself in the full-length mirror in the
changing room I still think it's my body that I'm seeing, not
somebody else's. I don't think, who's that old man who looks
like me?

I suppose Gabriel still looks much the same too. I suppose his
hair looks much the same, much the same as yours my darling.

Lunch.

What time is it?

plate 64 (opposite) 118
18 Brooke Street, London
1886–7

The Vail house is the climax of Richardson's townhouse
designs. The boldness with which he exploited the unpromising
corner site and the severity of the elevations seem all the more
remarkable when one considers that the architect never actually
saw Brooke Street, but worked entirely from drawings and the
written description of the future owner.[1]

The house was commissioned in 1884 by C.B. Vail, the wealthy
head of a Chicago engineering company, who had recently trans-
ferred his business to London, and he evidently encouraged
Richardson to develop the most forward-looking features of his
late work. The exterior detailing is minimal, and the use of
hammered granite, Old Red Sandstone and unglazed red tiles
increases the almost daunting plainness of mass and line. A
massive shallow arch protects the concealed front door, support-
ing a monumentally carved balustrade fronting the first floor
family rooms; the striking "blank" effect of the upper windows
is achieved by setting the sashes flush with the stonework. Only
the "Romanesque" tympanum carved with the family initials
provides any hint of the rich ornamentation of the interior; the
façade authentically evokes the vigour of Chicago's early steel-
framed multi-storied retail buildings, for many of which Vail's
firm had provided the interior engineering. He clearly expected
Richardson to make full use of current domestic and commercial
technology in his work; the lay-out of the house is largely determined by the innovative use of a concealed heating system and
of extensive soundproofing (which allowed, for instance, bedrooms and reception rooms to be placed on the same floor where
necessary).

Richardson's realisation that the internal structural logic of a
house could determine the drama of its exterior set a precedent
which was not to be fully realised for another thirty years. Frank
Lloyd Wright, acknowledging his debt to the radical townhouse

designs of Richardson and his contemporaries, referred to them as "the first modern buildings".[2]

On completion, the house was criticised for being both ugly and incomprehensible, and, significantly, for being an "inartistic" intruder into its aristocratic surroundings. One report described it as "a house with something to hide".[3] It is only with nearly a century of hindsight that the historic implications of the house's construction can be fully understood.

[1] Richardson/Vail correspondence, Richardson papers CC/12/85, Chicago Architectural Foundation

[2] Wright, ibid, p.247

[3] *The Studio*, London, January 1888

from *HENRY HOBSON RICHARDSON: A Pictorial Record*, William A. Neilson, Boston, 1971, (ill.)

I was twenty – younger than the century – I was a young man in London town, but if you had asked me, I would never have said that I was expecting anything. And I certainly wouldn't ever have said that I was expecting to meet him again. And certainly not on a weekday. And then there I was, coming out of work at five minutes past five, down in the lift and through Cosmetics and out through the side entrance in Duke Street, and there he was, standing right there on the other side of the street, in the middle of the pavement in the middle of the rush-hour in his beautiful great dark-blue cashmere coat. With the crowds parting either side of him and with his hand raised in a friendly wave.

This must have been in early March some time.

I stopped dead and just stood there; I couldn't really believe it. Not again. He must have seen from my face that I wasn't pleased, that I wasn't pleased to see him again after the fiasco at the theatre. He dodged through the queue of taxis on Duke Street and came right up to me and launched into his explanation at once. It was a coincidence, of course; how extraordinary, he'd just been doing some shopping, did I always finish at this time, I mean what else would a man be doing loitering outside Selfridges at closing time?

Well I couldn't help noticing that he wasn't carrying any parcels, and since the night of the theatre I had been doing some thinking. As he stood there talking at me over the noise of the Oxford Street rush hour I really was on the edge of saying look, Mr Clive, it's no good; I can see that you're not carrying anything. So this time you are going to have to give me an actual explanation, not just an excuse. Tell me why we keep on meeting like this. Tell me how you always seem to know where to find me.

Do you know my address? Are you going to turn up at my flat one day? And while you're about it, tell me why it is that you talk to me as if you have chosen me to be your closest friend and then you go and make a point of staging a big scene in the foyer of the London Pavilion where you talk to half the West End of London as if they were your friends and I know full well that they can't possibly be, not all of them. And for god's sake Mr Clive don't you ever, ever dare stand out here on the pavement outside work waiting to catch me when I come out ever again. Not right here on Duke Street where somebody from the Department might see us and ask me who you are and do I know you and quite frankly what am I expected to say in reply to that Mr Clive? "I hardly know him but I know everything there is to know about his house"?; or, "We First Night together but he's always gone by the time the houselights come up"?

Of course I never did say any of that. He saw me looking at his empty hands and he was out with his answer before I had time to ask the question; "Well, I say I've been shopping, but actually I've been ordering things again. I tell you, by the time the thirteenth comes around and the money comes in I sometimes think I shall be almost spent up! Look, shall we get out of here – let's go somewhere a bit quieter shall we?'

Of course. Of course he wasn't carrying anything. I should have never expected that he would be; customers like him always had their parcels delivered and they still do. Cashmere, the finest gloves – and no parcels. How silly of me to have thought otherwise. How silly of me to have even suspected him of lying to me. Of course there was a reasonable explanation – and no sooner had he finished it than Mr Clive gave me his best smile. That was always his trump card, and he knew it. When he smiled at you, smiled as if seeing you was a sudden, unexpected pleasure, you had to believe whatever he was saying. He was like that. When he talked, you listened. And when he took firmly hold of my elbow and guided me through the noise and the traffic and the rushing of Oxford Street and down Duke Street towards Brooke Street, well, I went with him. I let him take me. Out of my world and down into his.

I wonder what he had been ordering? The tickets? The suitcases? The two fur coats for when they got there and found it was still snowing?

At that time of a March evening the streets of Mayfair are almost completely empty, and just beginning to darken. On the W1 side of Duke Street all the shop windows were still alight; all the great displays of crystal and Royal Doulton on marble-topped tables, and all with no prices marked. Shops where you could buy everything you needed for a house like his – on credit, if you had an address like his, and a voice like his. Then suddenly there was the great empty space of Grosvenor Square, the plane trees still leafless and the earth still all black and bare that year as I remember it. Across to the west and down at the end of Upper Brooke Street you could see the sun setting over the park, the sky completely clear and turning from blue to red to black as you watched. We were both walking fast, because it was exactly that time when you can feel it getting colder by the minute, and as we approached the north-east corner of the square I suddenly thought that this time it was going to be different; he was going to hurry me out of the crowds and the cold and into the heat and the silence of Brooke Street and take me into the front room and sit me down and finally tell me everything. But when we reached the north-east corner of the square we turned right, not left, and crossed over, so that we were walking right up against the high black railings. Eight or nine times we must have walked round it; every time we came to the north-east corner I was sure that this time he would turn off and lead me down Brooke Street to number eighteen, and every time we just kept on walking, heads down, till the square was so dark that you couldn't see across it, and the lamps were all coming on one by one by one.

For a long time Mr Clive didn't speak, which was partly what had made me think he was going to take me back to number eighteen – I thought he was rehearsing the speech he was going to make when we got there, the confession. But then when he did start to talk he picked up exactly where he had left off the last time we had met; almost in mid-sentence. And it wasn't even as if he was talking to me, exactly; he just talked. Looking down at the pavement, mostly, or up across the empty square, but not where he was going, and certainly not at me. And in that particular kind of low, unstoppable voice that you hear from people on the street who really are talking to themselves.

It was all about money; how his hands were tied, how the staff were threatening to leave, how he'd been managing for months on the understanding that everything would be resolved on the evening of the thirteenth, and how he had just been informed that the executors were unable to reveal the exact figures prior to his coming of age, so that now he wasn't even sure how much was going to be left, what his allowance would be, and how it was all some elaborate system to ensure that things would be run just as they had always been run – and then he stopped, just as suddenly as he had started. It was as if he had suddenly remembered that I was there. He took a deep breath, as if he'd got that all off his chest, and turned to me with his very best smile on and said, "Well, Page, I'm sure you don't want to hear about all of that. And how are you keeping?"

We were back at the corner of the square again; you could even see number eighteen from there. He asked me how I was, and had I enjoyed the show, and wasn't Miss Losch wonderful, and did I remember meeting so and so, what had I thought of him – and it did cross my mind that actually he was stalling, "making conversation" – he even looked up the street towards number eighteen – and I'll swear that he winced when he looked at it. And then, as if he could tell what I was thinking, he gave his little laugh to himself and said, "Oh dear, Mr Page; I'm rather afraid I need to get just a little more air before I go back to all that. Tell me, did you ever hear any of those stories about Viscount Harcourt, Mr Page?"

No, I said, no I hadn't.

"Number twenty-two, just along from us" – and he waved in the general direction of Brooke Street, which was behind us again now, because he'd turned the corner and set off down along the railings again. He'd obviously forgotten that he'd asked me all this once before.

"Some people say he went out of the second floor window –

though personally I heard that he was actually found in bed. Found in bed by the faithful valet. Ah, that staple of costume drama and society gossip, Mr Page; the staff. What would we do without them? I suppose I may be about to find out – Lord but it's bitter out here!"

He hunched his shoulders up against the dropping temperature and quickened his pace, leaving me two steps behind.

If someone had seen us like that, I wonder if they'd have thought that he was hurrying to get somewhere, or to get away from someone. Or that he was just trying to think, to work something out. Or just trying to keep warm.

"And how do you live, Mr Page? On your own? Parents?"

"No, on my own actually," I said, though it didn't matter what I said, because it wasn't me we were talking about – it is his voice that I remember. And it's the way he walked in that marvellous coat of his that I can still see – anyway, I didn't lie. I told him about having only been in London for just a year, about having a place of my own for the first time, that it was in NW1, and I told him that I didn't really keep in touch with my parents any more – and that made him stop and look at me again.

"Ah; so you see, Mr Page, we are the same, aren't we?"

I asked him what he meant, I suppose.

"Don't tell me you've never noticed Mr Page. Somebody at the Pavilion even asked if you were my brother. Of course I told them at once that you were my long lost twin – " and he spun round and took hold of me by my shoulders, just like the first time that we'd ever met. I think he wanted to see how I'd react.

" – Only joking, Mr Page. But you could be, don't you think? I'm sure Mr Cochran thought you were. You *are* five foot ten in your stockinged feet, aren't you? There you are you see, I thought so. Quite remarkably alike – *uncannily* alike is how I'd put it. Has it never crossed your mind, Mr Page – all these odd little similarities, I mean? Never given you pause for thought?"

He was holding me much too tight for it to be a joke, and he had his face right up close to mine. I think he realised that he had gone too far; he grinned, let go of me, and took my arm again, and led me on, and we were just two gentlemen out walking in the Mayfair dusk again, nothing odd about that at all, Officer, and his voice went back to how it was before, that effortless West One voice that could talk all night and that no one in that part of town would ever think of commenting on.

"All the staff are threatening to leave – did I say that? It rather looks as if I am going to be left all alone with just that boy who arrived on Christmas Eve. He's the only one of all of them who seems not to mind about the delay with the money. Grateful for the work I suppose, although I do sometimes wonder if he quite understands the situation, since he barely speaks even Berlitz School English. All alone with someone who never says a word, Mr Page, just imagine. And can I buy a dictionary anywhere? Not in Selfridges, I am sorry to say. Not even for ready money. They did offer to order me one but I'm afraid I really can't wait ten days at this point in time."

Was that the young man with the white hair, I asked.

"Blond, Page, blond. Apparently it's quite common where he comes from. 'Balt', he calls it. As in Baltic Sea. White sea; white hair. So, left to fend for oneself on credit with a blond who doesn't understand a single thing that you want him to do for you; what would you do, Mr Page?"

And then he waited for me to answer his question. Waited what felt like a full minute.

And I couldn't. It was my turn to wince.

Of course I couldn't. It was no use asking me. I could no more have told him what to do than I could have contradicted a customer at work or shouted at them.

He repeated the question, very slowly, so that I could see each word, that's how cold it had got. "What would you do, Mr Page? What would you do in my situation?"

It was no good him repeating himself like that. There's nowhere in Grosvenor Square that you can't be seen from at least a hundred windows when the trees are leafless like that, and on a cold clear evening like that sound carries right across it if you raise your voice. Of course I couldn't answer his question.

"I mean you work with accounts, don't you, Mr Page? Accounts, sums, bills, figures? What would you advise a gentleman to do under these circumstances and in this day and age? Oh come on, Page, I can't stand here all night.'

I can see him now, standing there in the great empty square with the lamps coming on behind him, waiting and waiting for my answer and never once taking his eyes off my face, and then him suddenly taking a step back and throwing out both his arms like a scarecrow and throwing his head right back and shouting, so loud that I swear he made Grosvenor Square echo, WHAT THE HELL AM I GOING TO DO.

And I didn't know. I didn't know anything. I didn't know anything except that we shouldn't have been talking like that out in the open. That it shouldn't have been me that he asked, that I should have gone straight home, that I should never have accepted his invitation in the first place. And that it should have been spring by then, that the earth shouldn't have been that black, the air shouldn't have been that cold, the trees shouldn't have been so bare, and he should never have asked me, never have picked on me in the first place.

I did the only thing I could think of. I took a step towards him and I put my hand over his mouth. I don't know what on earth possessed me to do it; I just had to, I suppose.

"Please don't raise your voice," I said.

When I write it down like that then I can see now whose mouth I was actually putting my hand over. Not his. I was giving him the good advice Mr Page was going to spend the next thirty years giving himself, saying to him what I was going to be saying to myself almost every day of my life on the top deck of the number twenty-nine, please don't raise your voice, don't look, don't make a fuss, don't, please. Please wait until no one is looking. Wait until we get off the bloody bus. Wait until we get round the corner at least. Wait until I've locked the door. Please let me just make sure the door's locked. Wait a minute. Wait a minute, wait thirty years. Thirty years, Mr Clive.

When I took my hand off his mouth, we were both breathing heavily, almost as if there had been a fight. He looked exhausted; he even wiped the back of his hand across his mouth as if he was wiping the blood away from a split lip.

"Thank you, Mr Page," he said quietly. "Why don't you come back to number eighteen with me and I'll get him to bring us plenty to drink and then perhaps you'll be able to think of something. And I promise not to raise my voice."

No, I said, I couldn't. I couldn't possibly. I had to get home myself.

He could see then that he'd scared me. He patted me on the shoulder, and said goodnight –

"I'm sorry, Page; you're right. Time to go home. Time to go home and – have another meeting with the Family Solicitor."

He turned his back on me and walked away. I watched him, and as he went he said, without turning round, "Why don't you come to dinner one night and we'll continue our discussion? Why don't you come to dinner, Mr Page? Go on, be a devil!"

I looked down, and then suddenly I couldn't see him – he must have cut through a gate in the railings. There are no lamps in the middle of Grosvenor Square, and in that dark blue cashmere he literally just disappeared into the night. I could hear him starting to laugh, and starting to shout things, shout to the whole square, to the whole of West One, using my name so that I was sure everybody could hear it right up as far as Oxford Street.

"How about next week, Page? It's our birthday, remember?" – and he was singing now, hidden somewhere in the darkness, " – twenty-one today, twenty-one today, I've got the key to the door, never been twenty-one before – " I listened and listened and eventually I thought that was it, he'd gone. But then the moment I turned to make my own way home he spoke at me again; he must have been watching me. I couldn't see him but from somewhere out there in the darkness in the middle of Grosvenor Square his voice came straight to me, clear and hard and collected.

"I can see you! The key to the door, Page; you've got the key to the door, and don't you forget it. Number eighteen, March the thirteenth, this year of grace, 1924, remember?"

He started to whistle the tune of the song; the whistling turned to laughter again, and then that died away too. I watched carefully to see if I could spot him walking out of the other side of the square into the light of the streetlamps, but he seemed to have vanished entirely.

A clear sky like that, in March, can bring a frost even right in the middle of town. Even though it was the long way round I walked south, and went home via Piccadilly, through the lights of Piccadilly and Leicester Square and down into the Northern Line. I think I needed to be in a bit of a crowd. Even when I got home I couldn't get myself warm.

1924. Me sitting there huddled over the gas and him sitting alone in that front parlour. Throwing his coat on a chair and shouting for someone to bring him something hot to drink. Ringing the bell and having Gabriel make a fire up for him even though the heating was on full. Watching Gabriel kneel down and work at the fireplace in his perfectly cut black trousers. Then watching the firelight beginning to glow on all the glass and the china and the buttons on Gabriel's jacket, and making the hairs turn gold on the back of his neck. And then Mr Clive having to say to him *thank you Gabriel, that will be all.*

And then him sitting there and staring into the fire. And then not being able to stand the silence in the room any longer and getting up and putting on the radio or a record, that record of Sonnie Hale singing "Dance, Dance, Dance" – or maybe "Poor Little Rich Girl"; that would have been perfect, that would have made him laugh, I'm sure. I can just see him standing there in the middle of the room playing it again and again, laughing. And his laugh turning into a howl. Because he knows full well that no one's going to come. No one can hear him; the boy can't hear him unless he rings, not with those double floors. He can curse him or whisper the filthiest things he wants or call his name out loud in the middle of the night and he won't hear a single word of it. He can stand there sobbing, sobbing and biting his lip, oh, I can just imagine it. That terrible silence which only happens when you long for someone else to be there, for someone else to make a move or make a noise. And now here I am sitting all alone staring at my fire, only mine's gas, and staring at the snow scene, only it's hanging on my wall now, not his. And do you think that when he asked me that, *what would you do in my situation, Mr Page*, do you think that that wasn't already a familiar question to me? And do you think that when I hear him shouting it at me now across the darkness of Grosvenor Square after all these years that I haven't been thinking about it ever since? And do you think that I haven't asked myself that question a lot? When I am lying there wondering if the dream will come again, or when I am at work, trying to care about what I am doing and concentrate properly, or when I see the things in the papers, or when I am sitting here in front of the gas, sitting, just sitting, just staring at all those people in the snow, do you think that isn't exactly what I still say to myself? Sometimes I even say it out loud. Yes, I actually sit here on my own with no one else here and I say it right out loud, *well, Mr Page*, I say, *what should you do, in your situation?*

Looking back I do sometimes wonder who that young man was, that man with his hand over Mr Clive's mouth in Grosvenor Square, in 1924.

All over the shop, that's what people say, which is quite wrong, because things at work were the opposite of confused, or a mess; there were things all over the shop, but every single one of them was in the right place and I always knew exactly where that place was. We had everything and anything in those days, every day a new product or promotion or feature – the White Sale, the Fur Sale, the Election Night parties, all the latest. The biggest area of plate glass in the world, the Information Bureau – "An Answer to Every Question". Perhaps I should have sent Mr Clive there.

At the time I think I was a bit shaken, but I was too busy, in a way, to spend too much time worrying, too distracted, that's it. Mr Selfridge was always making some speech about bigger and better and newer, and I loved all that. Mr Selfridge, standing next to Gordon Selfridge Junior in his top hat and making a speech about the coming generations and so on. He was always showing him off, the son and heir. I wonder if Mr Clive ever met him, or knew him? – he probably did. On Election Night, for instance, you did get a lot of Society people there, wheeled in for the papers, and always there'd be a gang of young men "down" for the night, drinking too much and talking too loud. There'd be a band, and speeches, and then very late on you would have Lady Curzon or the Grand Duke Michael arriving, or Fay Compton making her entrance in some wonderful fur. Or the Dolly Sisters with Mr Selfridge himself, all chinchilla and emeralds – now that *was* in the papers. And all of the staff were expected to be there to swell the crowd – and to work, of course. *A Full English Breakfast Will be Served* – chicken and fruit salad and champagne for the guests all night, and then we would dish up bacon and eggs at three o'clock in the morning as the results were coming in – and that was when you would get the University people arriving, very drunk, for their breakfast. Maybe I even served Mr Clive bacon and eggs at three o'clock in the morning without knowing it. I probably said to him, there you are, sir. *There you are.* Was that when he discovered the only other man in the whole of London who looked like him? The only other man in the world who was actually, precisely, in his situation?

When the results came in there were these giant thermometers, and when a new result was announced another red bulb would light up, and everybody would cheer. I can't remember any of the names of who won or who lost or why. That wasn't really what I was interested in, never has been. Miss Compton in her colobus coat was more my sort of thing. I don't mean to say I was begrudging, or not excited to be in the middle of a cheering crowd, to be working in the middle of London, at one of the most famous addresses in the world. It's just that I didn't – I wasn't very good at questions in those days. Well now, now I want to know. I want to get it all sorted out before I go back to work. I'll stay up all night if I have to.

··············

I love timetables. Something about working with columns of figures all the time, I suppose; to me they're more than that. A timetable can really set me off; I like to sit here and choose which connections to make, which destinations to book for, all the journeys you could ever want to take, all those beautiful names of the places you've never been to and never will now (I never have been abroad myself, I mean not as a traveller, only in 1943 and 1944). When I sit here and read the columns of figures I can imagine myself looking out of train windows and seeing it all slide past, deciding whether to change at Vienna and head north into the cold, or to head south for Palermo where the spring has probably already started. Menton, Firenze. Narcissi; mimosa.

According to *Cook's Travel Guide and Timetable for 1923–24* there was only one ship coming in to London from the White Sea that got here at the time which Mr Clive specified, which must have been some time during the late afternoon of Christmas Eve itself. There was a train, which would have got him to Victoria that evening at the end of a four-day journey (Riga, Kovno, Wirballen, Berlin, Cologne, Brussels, Ostende, London, a sleeper line, no changing necessary, but that would have cost him nearly twice as much as coming by sea). So here it is; the S.S. *Baltabar* (should that be *Balthazar*? Is that *Balthazar* in his language?), coming from Riga to London direct, The United Baltic Corporation Limited, arriving Hay's Wharf, Tooley Street, 4.23 p.m., twenty-fourth. There is a note to say that not even that winter of 1923 could have prevented the boat from arriving on time; if the river wharf in Riga was frozen then there was a train laid on to take Gabriel to the coast, and there the S.S. *Baltabar* would be waiting to plough and smash an easy path out through the sea ice, so that that way he could be sure that his ticket would bring him all the way to the Thames, right up into the Pool of London as darkness fell, up to Tower Bridge, right up past all the steeples of the City churches as they started to ring out for Christmas Eve. That sounds like the one to me.

People still talk about that winter – they even mentioned it on the radio. It must have been one of those nights when the river is very still, and they say the water gets cold enough to kill you if you fall. Dangerous; like black glass. And now here is the steamer coming up out of the darkness and right in under Tower Bridge, and here comes the snow, starting to fall right on cue as it sounds its horn, so that when you look up from the wharf into the lights underneath the great metal ribs of the bridge you can see that amazing sight that always makes you feel like a child again; pure white flakes dropping out of a pitch black sky. That's what everyone really wants for Christmas – even after all these years.

After the waiting and waiting, especially in that sort of cold, it seems impossible that the timetable could be so exactly right, that the ship could suddenly be there looming up out of the dark so exactly on time. It has come so far, through ice, across a whole sea and from some place that you've never even heard of; but then there it is, unbelievable, S.S. *Balthazar*, and suddenly the whole wharf is shouting, bags are being thrown down, papers are being hurriedly checked (my god, but it's cold now), one woman is shouting and shouting in a language you didn't know people in London spoke, she's spotted the person she has been waiting for all these hours or maybe years. And on Christmas Eve too! People are being grabbed and hugged and hurried off to get the last bus across London to whatever Christmas celebrations have been prepared in their honour, the spare room cleaned and decorated and the table all laid. And Gabriel – the way I see it – Gabriel is the last to get off the boat. He is always alone, that boy. There he is, coming slowly down the gang-plank now, with the snow thickening around him and settling on his hair, and the lights from the bridge are catching him so that he looks like royalty arriving in a newsreel – except that there is no crowd to greet him.

Though he is expected.

After the war, when everything re-opened, somebody took me to see one of the first performances of *Swan Lake*. You have to remember that there hadn't been colours or music like that for years. That bit where the Enchanter's music comes in, and you see the lake itself, the blackness of the water, and then the swans all come on for the first time, I'll never forget it. And the thing was you see I didn't think there was anything magical or odd about it; with the black water, and their white feathers, all I saw was swans, not dancers at all. Where I came from as a child we were quite close to the Severn, and when the snow came, that was when the swans came down on to the river. And my mother would always tell me that they had flown all the way from Russia. *Look, here they come*, she'd say, *look*. And I can remember her holding me, and looking up into the snow as it fell, and not understanding how she could possibly know that they were coming – because they came every year, on time, just like a ship arriving. I'd stare hard up into the snow like I was told to, blinking as it caught my eyelashes, and stung, and melted, and then one flake spinning down towards me would be larger than the rest, and then suddenly, impossibly, the piece of snow would burst into a great white bird, opening its wings at the very last moment and settling silently on the water just the way the snow did. Birds falling out of the sky. Travelling by a timetable that only they knew about and bringing all the cold and the darkness with them. So whenever I hear that music now, or when I'm reading the column of figures, *arriving Hay's Wharf 4.23 December 24*, that is all in my mind too, so that when I see Gabriel walking down a gangplank he is also a bird, coming out of the snow, landing in a foreign country. Now that all the crowd of passengers has gone (you'd almost think he was a castaway; it's almost as if he doesn't *want* anyone to see him leave the ship), it must be five o'clock, because listen, all the bells of the City of London are announcing that there are only seven hours left until Christmas itself, the shops are shutting all over town, even on Oxford Street, and as St Paul's itself rings out he folds up his great wings (his *pinions*, that's the word) with one great final swirl of feathers and tucks them up under his cheap black overcoat so that no one will know who he really is.

There are no clues as to all the things he is about to make happen – nothing except that extraordinary whiteness of his hair. He walks to the immigration desk with one hand gloved, holding a small, battered suitcase, and one hand bare, holding a precious scrap of paper; on the paper is typed the address which is the only thing he has to guide him through this foreign city. His face is white with cold and, I suppose, with excitement.

Now I suppose on Christmas Eve things may have been a bit slack, officials eager to get home and so on, but still it says quite clearly here that he would have had to have had a guarantee, in writing, of his employment prospects in London, from the Minister of Labour here in London, before he could land. This is all set out quite clearly under RULES FOR ALIENS, country by country.

In other words Mr Clive would have had to have offered him the job at Brooke Street before he got here, in writing, and to have organised the permit for him.

None of which I knew until I looked it up here.

None of which Mr Clive told me. In fact, he gave me the clear impression that Gabriel had arrived at number eighteen more or less by accident. I should have seen it, of course. It should have been obvious; with no money and practically no English (none that I ever heard) how could Gabriel possibly have crossed London, got on to the books of one of those very superior staff agencies in Duke Street or South Audley Street, and been taken on, all in time to be found by Mr Clive at a quarter to seven, on Christmas Eve, polishing the Georgian silver, for a party that never happened? Mr Clive just wanted me to believe that that was what had happened, that he had just opened a door and there Gabriel was, the faithful valet, just the man he had been looking for – that was what he called him, the man who worked for that Viscount Harcourt, "the faithful valet" – and on Christmas Eve, too – a gift. Or did Mr Clive say that because actually that was how he wished it could have been, thought it should have been? Was that the way he wished meeting the man he had been looking for could have happened?

But Gabriel must have had *some* English money; he must have taken a taxi. How else could someone who couldn't speak English have crossed London in the snow in less than two hours? What on earth must Gabriel have thought, if the first thing he saw of London was seen from the windows of a taxi on Oxford Street on Christmas Eve just after all the stores had closed; all those blazing windows and the lights up on the front of the House – what was it that year? Soldiers? Snowflakes? Swans? I wonder if he was riding west just as I was going east on the number twenty-nine – I wouldn't have walked that night; there was too much snow, and anyway, I would have wanted to get home as soon as I could, to start getting myself smartened up for drinks with this strange and extraordinary and very wealthy man who I had just met. West along Oxford Street the taxi must have gone; left on to Gilbert Street, then right, the view of Grosvenor Square, and then along Brooke Street and there you are, sir, number eighteen, you can't miss it. The roof is red, the walls are of red stone, and there is the golden light just showing through the front door. It's warm inside – hot, even; and as I said, you're expected.

Mr Clive had ordered him. Maybe even ordered him to arrive just in time for Christmas, so that he really was his present, a present that he'd ordered and had delivered by taxi on Christmas Eve. Ordered. Just like his grandmother had ordered all the things for the house. You wouldn't think that things like that could just be ordered from a catalogue, because they look too precious, too beautiful. But they can be, you know. Anything the customer wants.

What sort of a catalogue did he find Gabriel in? Was it illustrated?

It sounds terrible when you put it like that. But if you think it sounds terrible then you have to remember Mr Clive's question, the one that he asked me, and then you have to tell me how you would have answered it. Would you have told him to wait? Wait until the spring came? But you see I don't think anyone should have to wait. No one should have to wait before they meet just the person they are looking for. Because for instance if I hadn't had to wait then we would have had longer together. There would have been more time, more Saturdays and more dinners and more times in front of the fire and that's what I want, oh that's what I want, that's what I want for Christmas, not to be sitting here alone reading a timetable, not to be sitting here alone looking up at the painting, not to be thinking about whether they ever made it or not. Because you do sometimes wonder, don't you. Half the journeys set out here in the timetable are ones you can't even make any more. Not since the start of the war, and certainly not since it ended. If you look on a map now, that dotted line which was the route Gabriel's ship took is gone; the sea is blank along that coast. You can still sit and read the list of all the things in that city in March 1924, but you can't be sure if any of them are still there. The tennis club for foreigners, the railway station with platform announcements for trains to every capital city in Europe. And next to the Opera House, the public gardens, and Otto Schwarz's café, strongly recommended to the English tourist for the taking of five o'clock tea. Perhaps that's where somebody saw him, aged nineteen, with his white hair, working as a waiter. Somebody saw his white hair, and smiled, and told him all about London.

Everything goes out of date. Timetables, catalogues. Things you thought would always be there go. Whole countries go. The sound of someone in the next room.

God knows what Mrs Welch thought all the noise was that

first afternoon. She never did say anything. All that noise and then bacon and eggs in the middle of the night.

Which is more than I'll be getting tonight. I should have got more in.

I suppose I could just sit here with the gas full on and the brandy open and my timetable open and my dressing gown open and that'll be some sort of a Christmas. Brandy and Memories. How does that sound Mrs Welch? Is that how you're imagining me? Sitting up all day and half the night. *Really well what a funny way to keep Christmas Mr Page I'm sure, I had no idea.* I'm sure you didn't Mrs Welch. No one did. None at all. No one at all. Nothing on at all, Officer, not a stitch. Nothing to eat but plenty to drink, oh but Mr Page, didn't you fancy a nice bit of the bird cold and the pudding warmed over, well actually Mrs Welch you see I forgot the pudding, but fortunately I didn't forget the brandy, and frankly I don't give a damn because when you get to my age and when you've had the sort of a year that I've had all you're really bothered about is the brandy never mind the pudding Mrs Welch, never mind the pudding at all.

Oh we felt as though we were drunk.

What time is it?

That first time, it felt like being drunk. I mean we weren't actually drunk, it was the middle of the afternoon after all, but that was exactly how he made me feel. You know; bold. And have you ever had that happen to you, Mrs Welch, have you ever felt that, felt in that one single moment that there's absolutely nothing you can do – and then you never do get round to making him anything to eat, not until three in the morning anyway, because he said to me what time is it and I said it's the middle of the afternoon and he said isn't it time we were in bed then. Oh and all that noise we made.

Isn't it time I was in bed? What time *is* it now?

I could just go to bed. I could put this away and go to bed and in the morning clear the bottles away, put them in the back of the cupboard to keep for next year, shave, dress, get ready for Wednesday and then go back to work. Go back to the New Year as if I hadn't been doing any of this. Make that my New Year's Resolution. Just stop, now. Now. It's time you were in bed. After all, you never broke down. You never let yourself down, you never said a word to anybody. You left the house quickly and quietly and you never went back. You shut the door behind you and you never went back. And so why now. Why. Oh look at that handwriting, all over the shop. That hardly looks like my hand-writing at all. You can hardly get me on that, Officer. I mean, you just compare that writing with my signature at work, I think you'll find it hardly matches at all. You'll find that's hardly like me at all. Not like Mr Page at all. You wouldn't say I was the sort of person who would write that sort of thing down now would you?

forgive my bad writing darling I think perhaps the drink is beginning to

I don't want to have the dream again you see. Not with his eyes closed like that. That's why I am still sitting here at three o'clock in the morning writing.

Come back. Come back; come back, don't leave me alone tonight, darling, not tonight, please don't leave me alone tonight not again not tonight

No. 18 Brooke Street (next door but four to T.H. Wyatt's splendid Brooke House, home of the eccentric Viscount Harcourt) was by no means the grandest or largest of the Mayfair mansions of the 1880s, but it was certainly one of the most striking. It was built for Mr and Mrs C.B. Vail of Chicago, Illinois, by the great American architect H.H. Richardson, and completed just three months before his death in 1887. It is surprising that it was built at all; all rebuilding on the Grosvenor Estate was subject to the personal approval of the Duke, and it seems unlikely that a man who so admired the red-brick English Arts and Craftsiness of Duke and Gilbert Streets can have approved of or even understood Richardson's astonishing exercise in Chicago Romanesque. Doubtless the Vails' fortune had something to do with it; Vail was an acquaintance and colleague of fellow Chicagoan H. Gordon Selfridge, who was later to occupy one of the grandest of the lost Mayfair mansions, Lansdowne House itself.

The house was subject to much comment when first built; one wonders if Lady Bracknell was thinking of Richardson's stony, fortress-like façade when she mused, eight years after its completion, on the possibility of acts of violence in the vicinity of Grosvenor Square.

Number Eighteen had a strange and rather sad history. Mr and Mrs Vail occupied the house until Mr Vail's death in 1917, said to have been caused by the tragic double loss of his only daughter and her husband, Captain J.E.C. Vivian, in one of the earliest Zeppelin raids of the First World War. Mrs Vail then remained in the house with seven servants and her young grandson (to whom her late husband's touching memoir, "The Making of a House", had been dedicated), preserving its then-unfashionable splendours in aspic until her death in 1921. On his coming of age the grandson, Clive Vivian, described by *Vogue* in February 1924 as "one of our most strikingly eligible bachelors", chose to abandon the house, and to spend the rest of his life (and of the considerable family fortune) abroad. By 1924 the Depression was already on the horizon; Mayfair was full of empty property. It remained unoccupied; however, the remarkable Anglo-American interiors survived intact, except for the dispersal of the furnishings (including Mrs Vail's famous collection of glass and ceramics, some of which can still be seen in the Victoria and Albert Museum), and were fortunately photographed for *Country Life* in 1932. Six months later, the house was demolished to make way for the unremarkable sub-Lutyens commercial premises which now occupy the site.

Following the loss (except for a still-standing fragment of the original entrance) of the massive country house built in Bushey for the painter Hubert Herkomer in 1884, and scandalously bulldozed by Watford Council in 1939, nothing of Richardson's work now survives in this country. That of his two British buildings one should have been an artist's mansion, demolished to make way for a council estate, and the other a town house commissioned by a shop-fitter whose expensively purchased place in Society lasted only one generation, must surely earn his architecture some sort of strange distinction as a barometer of the cruelty and unpredictability of social change.

The London We Have Lost
Lucinda Clarke, Weathervane Books, New York, 1979, pp.31–2

Boxing Day

keeps on happening, and I want it to stop now. I want to keep to my routine more. I want the night to be the night, which is for sleeping, and the day to be the day, which is for clearing up and going back to work. Bad winters like this, you hardly know which is which, that's the trouble; how are you supposed to know what time it is? I want Christmas to be over and for it to be New Year already, this week in between is neither one year nor the other. I know it won't be new for me, nineteen fifty-six or -seven, I shan't hardly notice, nothing new about it except the figures, but that is what I want. I want to put all these things away back where they belong in the back of the cupboard. And then when I wake up and I draw back the curtains the place will be tidy and it will be light like it should be. And that gas is going off this time, so it will be cold, like it should be in the morning. And when I look at my watch it will be the time that it should be. Take this bloody dressing-gown off for a start, much too hot in bed in that, got all knotted up in it twisting and turning. Gown off, gas off, lights off, nice and dark, and I will be at home asleep in my bed not standing in the middle of Mayfair looking up. Not again tonight. Not looking up and seeing him in the sunshine with his eyes closed and then waking up and shouting Don't Don't Don't Leave Me Don't Jump, and all the time in the dream I'm thinking this is ridiculous because nobody jumped from the window of number eighteen, it was number twenty-two the man jumped from, and I didn't even know him, and anyway that was nineteen twenty-two, Mr Clive told me all about it. And then I'm looking down at my watch, it's two o'clock, the early afternoon of, etc, I'm crossing the street, the steps, and I'm ringing and ringing and ringing and then the door is already open, the stairs, the stair-carpet, the stair-rods, and then. Then the curtain and then that door is open too and then I am going down the corridor, which is further than I've ever got before, and then I find the bedroom, I get to the bedroom door, all these doors, and finally I'm standing in the bedroom doorway and "I would like a glass of water, please", I said. "It is so hot in here. I knew I should never have left that gas on. Could I have a glass of water please your Honour?" And they gave me a glass of water so that I could carry on with my evidence. *Could you speak up please Mr Page so that the court can hear you*, they said, because I was using a very tiny voice, a little boy's voice, because even before I got there I knew what I was going to find. I said to myself at the time, I said, I'm going to be able to see it, I'm going to stand in the doorway and I know full well I'm going to be able to see what's on the bed. And then the sound of the noise of the blood in my head starts. And now it isn't like a dream, it's like a film. I'm standing in the bedroom doorway, looking down at the bed, but I'm in a different place now. It's one of our Saturday afternoons, and I'm in the Empire Leicester Square, and it's packed. The only empty seat in the whole house is the one next to me. He hasn't turned up, he's late. And of course I'm worried about him. None of the other people in the cinema have any idea of what is going to happen next in the film, but suddenly I do, because I'm sitting there in the dark and watching it and thinking oh how disappointing I'm sure I've seen this one before and then I realise that this is a film of me going up the stairs, someone must have been watching me, and I know what it is we're going to see next, and I think, they can't be going to show that, not in a cinema, and I know without being told that I have to get out of there as quickly as I can before people realise that it's me. I think, if I can't get out, there's going to be trouble; but I can't get out, like I said it's packed, and I'm in the middle of a row, there are too many people, all in couples. They're starting to laugh now, and there's blood all over the place, I try not to look at what's on the screen, but I can hear the whole place laughing, and all I know is that I've got to stop the film somehow so I stand up on my seat even though I know they'll see me and I try to block out the beam of light with my hands and I start shouting for everybody to get out. Men never do scream in films, do they? Why is that? The way I remember it I wasn't able to make any noise at all, I was almost retching but there was nothing coming out of my throat, nothing coming out at all. No wonder I needed that glass of water. *Thank you, your Honour.* That's all I can remember, your Honour, honest. Can I go back to bed now please? And then when I woke up and looked down at my watch it said five o'clock. Five o'clock in the morning I suppose unless I have slept until it is dark again. Get that glass of water now and back to bed. You know he told you never to sleep with the gas on, you'll feel dreadful in the morning. Still no wonder you dropped off after all those stairs. Years it took, to get up those stairs, years.

Eleven o'clock a.m., December 26, 1956

Last night, in the middle of the night, I thought that I wasn't going to be able to stand it any more, but I wrote it down anyway, and now that it's morning, of course I can stand it.

I was drunk, that's all, and I'd left the gas on. And tomorrow, I'll be back at work. And so now I am going to write some more things down about what I am feeling and what I am thinking this morning.

What I would really like this morning would be to write this in bed for a bit, then to get up, go next door, and discover that the bathroom had been done up in the night. Brand new. Like a hotel bathroom, like Myrna Loy's, the Dorchester or something, or like the bathroom was at number eighteen. A whole pile of white towels all folded and waiting, that's my idea of luxury. And those white-tiled walls with the full-length mirrors. Silver taps. Unlimited hot water. So that it would be like having the London and Provincial Turkish up here on the fifth floor, right next door to my bedroom and all to myself. I'd get up and I'd spend a good couple of hours in there and wash everything away from last night. Let the taps run full blast, as hot as I could get them, steam all the mirrors up. And I'd have hand-made soaps, and English Fern Eau de Cologne in that wonderful green bottle, like he had. And when I was all done I'd wipe down one of the mirrors with one of the towels and take a good long look at myself. And I wouldn't be looking at all bad.

Then I would like to have lunch at Simpson's.

Then I would like to go to work (yes I know that the House is closed until tomorrow, but this is what I would like) and to have nobody recognise me. I'd like to be a customer, and in fact I'd like to be the only customer there – but all the staff would be there, waiting, and whatever I wanted to look at it would be *yes sir, certainly sir*. I'd go to the Ticket Bureau and choose a matinée, something musical – maybe even the ballet. I might even pop into the Travel Bureau and order some tickets to go away somewhere. Then I would walk home and stop off for tea on the corner of Poland Street, and the waiter with the forearms would bring it to me on a silver tray. A big pot of tea is just what I fancy. Hot tea usually does the trick. That and a good sweat, nothing like a good sweat to get the poisons out of your system.

Most of all of course I wish we were waking up together.

I have thought quite a bit about this, and I have decided that I am not going to use his name. I am not going to write it down I mean. His name I am going to keep just to myself. Because there are things that I do want to keep, that I very definitely do want to keep. Our waking up together. Our Saturday afternoons together at the cinema, or back here. The afternoons with the curtains drawn and the gas on. Then in the early evening being the first to wake up and lying there and seeing the clothes on the back of the chair and the pink walls and the gold lamplight and him still sleeping. The way he looked, sleeping.

The way he looked sitting across the table from me, that Christmas, which is four Christmasses ago now (though I keep on thinking it's so much longer). The way he picked up his knife and his fork and smiled and neither of us said anything. Well you don't, do you. Some things you don't talk about.

I would like him to come back just for one more dinner.

There you are you see you are writing a lot more down than you ever thought you would be able to. You can't write his name, but you can write all this about him, and you are not dreaming, and you are not crying any more. And it is sunny this morning. A sunny morning. That helps. Not that you can trust this December sunshine. The sun comes out, the ice starts to melt, but then it can snap back again without warning and the things that had started to shoot in the parks and gardens all blacken. It's not the food running out, it's the gas going off that I'm worried about in this weather. Running out of shillings. You tell yourself not to worry when the sun's out like this but come half-past four or five then this place could be freezing in no time at all. Is that always part of getting older I wonder, being scared of the cold? Of being able to feel the cold air coming off the window even though you've got it shut tight and the curtains drawn. The cold "getting to you", as they say, getting right into you, right there where you should be warmest and safest. Get indoors and get that gas on and you'll be fine I always tell myself. Lock the door, and when the place has warmed up a bit you can get those clothes off, no one'll see you. Oh I hate the cold, being cold, touching somebody's arm and it being cold.

Like I said, you can't trust the sunshine. Where was I?

··············

I've noticed that in proper stories you usually have a bit at the beginning of each chapter about how some more time has passed. Often the weather changes, or the daffodils or rhododendrons or the laburnum come into bloom at Manderley – that's how they usually do it. Well in March 1924 the weather didn't change. It stayed cold, and there were no spring flowers at all that year, not the way I remember it. Mr Clive must have been getting good at concealing the real state of affairs from his creditors by now, because he was still getting everything on tick, having everything delivered to the back door of number eighteen. He taught Gabriel to sign for things without saying anything to the tradesmen, so that no one would talk about the man with the white hair and the foreign accent, no one would ask themselves what on earth did that Mr Clive think he was doing having staff like that in the house? He spent all of his time in those last days just waiting, just counting the days and the hours; waiting to get his hands on his inheritance. He was rarely seen out in Society at this time. He found that he couldn't enjoy anything, couldn't keep his mind on anything any more. When *The Times* came in the morning there was nothing in it that interested him. He was even reduced to reading the reports of the weather at foreign resorts, that's how bored he was. And when the evenings came, he drank or stared into the fire or listened to record after record after record on the wind-up gramophone. Time did pass, but it seemed to him that it passed very, very slowly. The evenings he spent shut up in number eighteen were hell to him those first two weeks in March.

I don't *remember* any of that, of course. I don't *know* any of that. That's just what I imagine it was like.

And when the thirteenth of March finally came, he gave a dinner party.

I hadn't told anyone in the Department that I was going to be twenty-one that weekend – and I didn't know anyone else to tell. So I didn't have any celebrations of my own planned. And I expect I told myself some story about how it didn't really matter to me, but that I might as well have somebody else cook my birthday dinner. Or at least give me a drink. Or about how it would serve him right for shouting at me like that in the middle of Grosvenor Square if I took him at his word and turned up in the middle of his birthday party without having received a proper written invitation. I never admitted to myself how much I wanted to go back.

I was the first to arrive. I'd had to guess at the time, since Mr Clive hadn't been exactly specific about his plans for the evening, and I had decided that seven-thirty for eight had a proper sound to it. So knowing me it would have been seven-thirty exactly when I rang the doorbell of number eighteen. That's just how I was. Am. As I walked down Brooke Street and up the red steps to the front door I was looking forward to seeing Mr Clive's face when he saw me standing on his doorstep; to *him* being surprised to see *me* for a change. But when he opened the door he greeted me smiling, with a cigarette in his hand as always, and without the slightest hesitation.

"Ah, Mr Page," he said. "We knew that we could count on *you*. Do come in.'

That was it; no comment. He didn't even offer to take my coat, just indicated a chair for me to leave it on with an off-hand wave of his cigarette and walked away from me down the dark hallway and led the way up the stairs. As if he wanted to make a point that my turning up hadn't thrown him at all. He didn't even stop or turn round to address me directly when he said, halfway up the stairs, "Oh, and – Happy Birthday, Mr Page."

But either he wasn't as ready for his guests as he wanted to be, or he was past caring by this point in the story. You see the hallway of number eighteen was practically in darkness when I arrived – the golden window in the front door hadn't been glowing as it should have been, and what light there was on the stairs was coming from up on the landing. The shelf of glass vases was almost lost in the gloom – all I could see was one pair of plates that seemed to be able to collect what little light there was and shine even in the dark, like a pair of cat's eyes. Eyes that follow you across the room – or does that only happen with portraits? And it wasn't until we reached the landing that he flicked on a row of switches, and the bunches of electric lilies came blazing on all over the house, filling it with that odd, thick light, and turning the two glass plates back into a pair of round, blank, golden mirrors. And when he did that, I could see what sort of a state Mr Clive was in that evening, for all his smiling.

In the darkness of the hallway, Mr Clive had seemed as immaculate and as rude as ever – with his voice and his way of walking you always just naturally thought of him as being impeccably turned out. But now the lights were on you could definitely see that something was different – wrong, even. It wasn't that he was untidy exactly; it was just that every other time I had seen him he had been, well, perfect. He was wearing the sapphire cufflinks again that night, for instance, and the stones were as clear and perfect a blue as they ever were, but when he reached out his right hand to open the door to the front room I couldn't help but notice that the cuff of his evening shirt was filthy. It obviously wasn't a fresh one. I could tell that he was freshly shaved, because he was wearing cologne, in fact rather too much cologne, like you would if you had had time for a shave but not for a bath – but he had obviously shaved in too much of a hurry, because he'd nicked his neck. There was a small smudge of blood on the right side of his collar. As I walked behind him into the front room I could also see that he had missed a small patch on the back of his head when he had been brushing his hair. Not everyone would have noticed these things, but I did. I notice things like that you see, appearances. And that night I was determined to watch Mr Clive like a hawk, to really see what he was up to.

If it hadn't have been seven-thirty in the evening then I would have said that he looked as if he had just got out of bed.

He asked me what I wanted to drink, very formal, and gave me a sherry from the decanter on the sideboard. Then he walked to the window and carefully lifted the edge of one of the heavy drapes, just like he had done before, except that now he didn't manage to make it look half so casual. He made no attempt to make conversation with me, just smoked and smiled at me in a strained sort of way and gave a small, nervous version of his laugh to himself. He ran a hand through his unbrushed hair, and went to twist the gold ring, a signet, that he usually wore on his right hand – but he'd obviously forgotten to put it on. That mistake made him laugh to himself again. I thought he must be worrying about why the other guests were late, or even if they were going to come, and for a minute I must say I was rather enjoying the sight of him being stood up and inconvenienced for once. Then I saw the circles under his eyes, and a glitter in the eyes themselves that hadn't ever been there before, and it occurred to me that there might not be anyone else coming. That he was checking to make sure that we weren't going to be disturbed. That there might actually not be a party planned at all. After all, I had already noticed that there were no lights showing from the house that night, no signs of staff.

There was an awkward silence, with just a clock ticking. I said nothing, and he kept on looking at me in the oddest way. I drank my sherry. When I had emptied my glass, Mr Clive took a sudden step towards me, reaching out at me – and instinctively I took a step back. The next moment of course I realised that all he was going to do was re-fill my glass, and I felt a fool and said thank you and said yes I will have some more, it's excellent, thank you. Nevertheless as he had his back turned at the sideboard I was still – well I hadn't told anyone where I was planning to spend the evening, you see. And I knew that Mr Clive would have known that, he could have gambled quite confidently on the assumption that I would have had nobody to tell. So he could have planned to be alone with me. And if all the lights were off, so that no one passing would know that anyone was in, what kind of a celebration was he planning for our joint birthday? What had he meant when he had said *we knew we could rely on you?* Why had he been already smiling when he had opened the door?

I jumped so far out of my skin when the doorbell rang downstairs that I nearly dropped the glass as he handed it back to me, and when Mr Clive brought the first two of the other guests into the parlour to meet me I was still on my hands and knees trying to mop the sweet sherry out of the carpet with my handkerchief.

Mr Clive introduced us all to each other in that particular way that supposes that everyone knows who everyone is already. One of them I did know, actually – from the show at the Pavilion – a Mr Messel. The man with him seemed to know me or to have met me before, but I didn't recognise him. He asked me what I did, and when I said that I worked at Selfridges, he said *Oh, really?* as if that was something unusual. *Oh really, and in which Department?* I explained all that, and when I asked him what he did, he made a little pantomime of looking guiltily over his shoulder, lowering his voice into an elaborate sort of whisper and telling me that he worked *in the theatre*.

"I expect I was wearing a mask the last time you saw me," he said. "That's probably why you don't recognise me."

"Oh yes," I said. He must have been one of the boys in black suits in that number with Miss Losch – he had the most beautiful skin, nothing obvious, just very well cared for. And plucked eyebrows, which those boys always seem to have. The awful grins on those masks – that's what I must have looked like, that's what we all must have looked like standing there in the front room of number eighteen being polite to one another.

Every time the doorbell went Mr Clive left us and went downstairs to get it himself, which made me think that now there really were no staff at all in the house. I wondered if there were going to be any women at the party but by the time that five of the other guests had come it was clear that there weren't going to be.

When the sixth guest (another dancer, I think, from the way he held his head as if he was being photographed in profile all the time) had arrived, Mr Clive took us all into the dining room.

He threw open the double doors, doing his magician act again, and it was all I could do not to gasp.

Because it was like magic.

No one had come in to announce that dinner was served, I hadn't even seen Mr Clive check his watch or press a concealed bell, and yet when he opened the doors all the candles on the dining-room table were already lit. And so many of them – twenty, at least, or maybe there were actually twenty-one, and all in what looked like cut-crystal candlesticks. So many that the air was already dancing with the heat.

I had never seen anything like Mr Clive's table on that final night, not even in the very best of the windows at work. Eight thousand handkerchiefs, in every colour of silk and lace ever made – a live monkey perched on a treasure chest of costume jewellery – a jungle of chandeliers all lit in the middle of the afternoon – they can be very wonderful; but nothing the Display Department has ever done was as wonderful as that great table ablaze with candles and the champagne already on ice and everything, everything made of gold.

There were eight chairs, eight places laid, and mine was at the foot of the table, so that I was sitting facing Mr Clive. Each place had a small label, in a gold clip, with the guest's name on it; mine said just *Mr Page* – I never did tell him my Christian name. That made the blood come into my face for a moment; I was angry because he had just assumed that I wouldn't have had any alternative plans for the night of my twenty-first birthday, and I was angry because he was right. He knew me so well, and it wasn't as if we were – I mean, it's not as if we were exactly friends. If anyone had asked me, I would have said that I was ashamed. Ashamed that I was so – easy. That he could tell. That it showed. But no one did ask me, of course; nobody knew anybody else well enough for anything except polite conversation. I don't think anyone quite knew why they had been invited; I quickly realised that I wasn't the only one who had expected everyone else except themselves to be close friends of Mr Clive's, when in fact it was quite obvious that none of us were. Acquaintances, that was the best you could say. Eight men seated round a table with only one servant may sound all very intimate, but it wasn't. The reason why we all got so drunk that night was because everyone was so on edge, not because anyone had anything to celebrate.

Mr Clive was the last to sit down, at the head of the table, and as he sat down suddenly Gabriel was there at his shoulder. Tonight Gabriel was wearing the black trousers and white gloves again, but this time with a jacket of dark blue, midnight blue, with real silver-bullion braid on the collar and four silver buttons at the cuff. In the light of the candles the buttons, the braid, and, of course, his hair all turned to gold. It was definitely a finale costume, something from the last act. The Ballroom Scene, when all the main characters have been assembled and midnight is about to strike. When he appeared, the dancer who had been trying to talk to me raised one of his plucked eyebrows and looked at me, but I didn't say anything, certainly didn't say *yes, I know, I've seen him before*. I didn't say anything, and neither did anybody else.

The whole evening was like that. There we were, we'd all been assembled for this special occasion, none of us were men who were backward in coming forward I am quite sure under different circumstances, and yet nobody said anything. Now, that sounds peculiar. Then, I didn't find it peculiar at all. I was grateful and I was relieved.

And then dinner was served.

Everything on the table was gold. Even the food. Butter (already melting in the heat), oil and vinegar – shining in a cut-glass cruet – the pale gold champagne that Gabriel kept on pouring us, golden hot-house grapes in a dish made of gilded vine leaves with a pair of miniature gold scissors attached by a length of golden chain. Gold fingerbowls. And wine-glasses that were gold too when you first looked at them, but somehow had all the colours of spilt petrol worked into the glass under the gold, and with stems so thin that I watched one of the other guests do it first before deciding that it was safe to pick one up. Each place had a green glass plate with flakes of what I suppose was real gold leaf in it, catching the light, and on each plate a starched damask napkin had been folded into an elaborate fan and tucked into a gold napkin-ring. This was flanked by five knives and five forks, all gold, and each setting had five of the golden glasses, all in different shapes – it must have taken someone a week to do all that. At least a week. To find which drawer each piece of glass or plate was in, to unwrap it carefully from the green baize cloth that it had been put away in, wash it properly, polish it using the correct cloth – and that linen; the ironing, the starching, the folding, getting each napkin exactly like in the illustration – because they must have used a book to do it. The gaps between each plate and the nearest wine-glass had been measured with a ruler, you could see that. It was better than the Christmas display in the China Department. In fact it was what the Christmas display tries to make you imagine.

All of that made the meal itself seem even stranger, because it was nothing like as grand or as careful as the table setting. For instance, we drank champagne all evening, with every single one of the courses, whereas I thought that when you had five different-shaped wine-glasses like that then the whole point was that you had a different wine each time. And the sequence in which the dishes were served seemed to have nothing to do with the way that the cutlery was laid out. If you had worked your way in from the outside, which was certainly what I was taught was the proper way to do it, then you would have ended up eating Russian salad with a dessert spoon and fish with a knife that was obviously meant for cheese and biscuits. The actual food was so strange that I am not sure that I can have remembered it right; Russian salad, lobster in mayonnaise, stuffed black olives, Bath Olivers, smoked oysters, more champagne, the grapes. And there wasn't much of anything – and it was all cold. Butter, but no bread; coffee, but no milk. Because only Gabriel was serving, there would be great long delays between one dish being taken away and the next arriving; and then when it did finally come he would get halfway round the table with something and then discover that there wasn't enough for everybody, and he'd have to disappear to get some more, so that half the table would be sitting there with empty plates while the other didn't know whether they should start, or wait, or what. Everybody did their best to keep on talking in order to fill in these gaps, and several of the men talked loudly and dropped the same names and laughed in the same sort of way that Mr Clive laughed, but still sometimes there wasn't enough conversation to go round either. You know how awful that can be, one moment everybody's talking, and then without anyone knowing why there is only one person talking, telling some story, and everybody else is listening, which is fine until they finish their story. And then Mr Clive would have to ask another question from the head of the table to get us all going again. I was always terrified he was going to ask me, stuck there at the end of the table as if I was the guest of honour or something.

Gabriel kept his white gloves on all the way through the meal, and sometimes you had not to look, because he had quite a struggle doing that trick of serving with both the spoon and fork in one hand, especially with things like the lobster, and his gloves were soon spotted with mayonnaise and other stains. Do waiters in the smart places always wear gloves? Was that correct? He served the dinner as if he had been practising but still hadn't quite mastered the art. If they had done it by looking up the "Dinner Party" chapter of some old book, something that had once belonged to Mr Clive's grandmother, then I think Gabriel hadn't been able to read it, or that Mr Clive hadn't explained it to him correctly, or there had been some pages missing.

By the time the coffee came round (that was cold, too) Mr Clive had drunk too much, and was having to work much too hard to keep the party going. In desperation, I suppose, he started telling us all the history of the house (and that was when I realised that possibly I had been here more often than some of the other guests; in fact, I've got no reason to think that any of them had ever been there before except me). He recited bits of his Guided Tour exactly as he had done for me, describing the different rooms in great detail and even pointing at things when he mentioned some notable object or feature, even though we were still sitting at the dining-room table. He did everything, the vases, the carpets, the picture of the snow scene hanging on the landing.

When he got halfway through the description of the heating system and how everything in the house was modern he gave his little laugh (and it sounded harder, and odder, than it ever had done before) and he looked straight at me. I was quite sure of what he was trying to tell me: *Don't say anything Mr Page. Don't say a word. I know you've heard all this before, I'm sorry about this, but please don't say anything. I promise you that I'll get to the point eventually. Let the fact that you've heard all this before just be our little secret, all right, Mr Page?* Mr Clive was very good at that trick of talking about one thing and meaning another, or thinking about something else entirely.

I didn't do much talking myself, largely because I didn't ever really want to take my eyes off Mr Clive. I was sure he was going to jump, or pounce, or come out with something terrible, and I wanted to be ready. To get out of the room, I think, if I had to.

Gabriel went round the table again, re-filling everyone's glass with champagne. We got through so many bottles that night you would have thought Mr Clive was trying deliberately to empty his cellar. When Gabriel had gone right round the seven of us he went to fill Mr Clive's glass too; but Mr Clive stopped him. He didn't do it by just putting his hand out over the top of the glass, palm down, which I know is how you are supposed to do it; he took hold of Gabriel's wrist. *No, thank you*, he said, quietly, almost under his breath, and looked up at Gabriel's face without letting go of his wrist. Their eyes met, and they just stayed there, face to face, eye to eye, right in front of everyone. Then, in one of the unlucky gaps in the conversation, he repeated himself, and this time everybody heard him; *thank you*. And when he said it this second time he said it right out loud, and the moment after he had said it his face twisted into a smile that wasn't like his usual smile at all; he looked hungry, is the only way I can describe it. Showed his teeth like a wolf. And his eyes were shining. *Thank you, Gabriel*, he said, a third time, still holding his wrist, and this time he knew perfectly well that everyone was looking and everyone was listening. And then without letting go of Gabriel he looked straight at me; so deliberately that one or two of the other guests also looked, wondering what on earth all this was about. And Mr Clive's glittering eyes were saying to me again, *yes, Page?*

Do you wish to say anything? Do you wish to comment on the situation? I thought you were the one who never says anything, Mr Page. Well?

Mr Clive let go of Gabriel's wrist and looked round the table at all of his guests. He picked up a fork, and began to knock it against the side of one of the golden wine-glasses – I was terrified that it was going to smash. There was no need for him to have done that; nobody was talking, everybody was staring at him anyway. The dancer person said *speech, speech.*

Mr Clive acknowledged him with a small wave of his hand and got unsteadily to his feet. He did it too quickly; he staggered, and had to clutch at the table to stop himself from falling. At once Gabriel was there, and caught him, and held him steady until he regained his balance. It was exactly like seeing the groom rise to reply to the speeches at a family wedding, and being too drunk to carry it off, except that this was even worse, because the bride in her dress and veil was actually having to help him stand up, not just sitting there quietly like she's supposed to. Those speeches are always so embarrassing. Just as well that most of the candles had burnt down and that we were all a bit flushed with the heat and the champagne, otherwise they would have seen that my face was burning.

"Gentlemen," he said, and my stomach went cold, because I thought, *this is it, yes, we are all gentlemen, we know that, we can all see that, please don't say anything –*

"Gentlemen," he said – and now this is Mr Clive's speech on the evening of the thirteenth of March 1924. I'll try to get it right.

Throughout the speech Gabriel was standing behind his chair, in his shadow, and Gabriel's face never moved, never showed a thing, even when he was referred to directly. Even if he spoke no or almost no English, I don't believe that he didn't understand what Mr Clive was saying. Or rather what he was getting at. Mr Clive's face was alive, more alive than I had ever seen it. He wasn't ever exactly handsome, but if you had seen him making that speech then you would never have said that he was plain. In that light his hair looked black, and his eyes had darkened too; under normal electric light his face would have been almost white I think, the colour you go just before you faint or vomit, but because it was lit from below by the light of the candles coming up off the white damask cloth, it was gold. Black and gold. I was sitting opposite him, remember, at the other end of the table, so that we were still face to face in a way, but now we looked very different. One of the twins was changing. Becoming un-like. Maybe it was just the champagne and the candlelight and the strangeness of the whole evening, but when he rose to make his speech, I was still Mr Page, but Mr Clive, Mr Clive looked like the Demon King.

"Gentlemen, I am sure you will all agree that sometimes one simply cannot stand it any longer. One simply cannot tolerate things carrying on as they are. I am for instance reminded tonight of my dear, late neighbour here in Brooke Street, whom some of you quite possibly had met and concerning whose sudden death eighteen months ago one has heard so many rumours. One does know how he felt, does one not. (I am getting this right; it was like that, very drawled, very drunk, very grand. You weren't quite sure if he was actually going to make it to the end of the sentence sometimes.) Some days, these days, one does ask oneself, What is one to do? The Pills? The Second Floor Window? Is it nobler in the mind to get on a train and leave town or to simply throw oneself under it? In the recent case to which I have alluded it seems we shall never know exactly how he actually did it. The only thing that seems sure is that he was found by his faithful valet. Perhaps he had no one else to turn to. Or to discover him, as it were. Which brings me to the terrible problem of staff. The terrible problem of staff. Terrible these days. (Like a toy drummer winding down. Then you turn the handle and it sets off again.) These terrible days. Nobody else to turn to; who would have thought it. Ah yes, in these terrible days, in these latter days, it came to pass, as the time approached, as the time drew near for me to assume my proper and indeed somewhat historic role as master of this house and to open it again to what can only be described, for want of a better term, as Society, my Grandmother being now dead and myself of, as they say, a proper age, I thought I had better at least try to do things properly. So important that, propriety, wouldn't you say, Mr Page? Wouldn't you say gentlemen? Well. Which leads me to the question of Staff. Staff. Staff are such a problem since the war don't you all find? Mrs Sandiman down in South Audley Street is in despair, I can assure you. Take my young friend here – (Gabriel, misunderstanding the way that Mr Clive had waved his arm in his general direction, came forward with the champagne bottle. Mr Clive took hold of him by his arm again and kept him there in the candlelight – I almost said *footlights*. So that we could all see him.) Gabriel here is really all I could get. (Now Mr Clive's voice changed; it was almost as if he had suddenly sobered up for a moment. He spoke very deliberately and calmly now, as if he was making sure that we all understood exactly what it was he was saying.) Gabriel has come to us all the way from the Baltic, gentlemen. Or the White Sea, as I understand it is to be properly called if we are to translate its name into our own tongue. I am sure that you will all agree that he is indeed a worthy and remarkable addition to the decorative scheme of the house. And, like the house itself, so practical, too. Several of you, I can't help having noticed, have been drawn to gaze upon Gabriel's hair. He himself assures me, in his as yet rudimentary English, that where he comes from hair such as his is common. White gold from the White Sea, one might say. (Here I remember him looking slowly round the table, looking each of the guests in the eye in turn, as if daring each of us in turn to interrupt or contradict him.) Gentlemen, when I knew that this old monster of a house was going to be mine I considered re-decorating it entirely, bringing everything up-to-date, as it were. I'm sure you know the sort of thing. Out with the old, in with the new, and somebody from the Tottenham Court Road to advise me on the furniture and so on. However, since Gabriel joined me here I have decided that white hair and white gloves are the only up-to-date features that the old place really needs. I intend him to be my sole contribution to the future life and reputation of this house. He is to be the finishing touch, as it were.

"Because, gentlemen (and now his voice rises again, because now he is really getting to the point, now he really is going to say what he means), because, gentlemen – well, not to bore you with the financial details, I am afraid that Gabriel is all the re-decoration I can afford.

"Tonight is, as you know, a very special night both for me and for this house – which is why your good selves have been invited here. Tonight is the night, you might say. Yes (looking straight at me but as if by accident, my stomach turning over). Twenty-one Today, gentlemen. The sad part is that the key to the door, regrettably, is just about all I have got. There isn't much else left. And after a spread like this, gentlemen, I should be rather surprised if there is anything left at all. I am of course sorry to disappoint those of you who came here tonight to not only celebrate my good fortune but also to investigate further any opportunities you might have of helping me spend it; but the fact of the matter is that the family solicitors inform me that not a penny remains. Well, a few pennies, but I'm afraid – I'm afraid I have done rather a lot of shopping in the last few months.

"Terrible days, as I did start off by saying, gentlemen. Terrible days of scandal, and of headlines, and of people who shall remain nameless.

"So, to conclude, tonight's little gathering is not to be, as I had originally hoped it might be, the first of many. It's rather a case of dust-sheets at dawn, I'm afraid. It was, I hope you'll agree, quite a show, but the notice has just gone up. Tonight's the last night, the band has already gone home, Gabriel here is the last surviving member of the chorus, and I'm afraid that this is the very last of the champagne. Quite frankly, it's a disaster."

(He said this word as if he loved saying it; repeated it to himself, swilling it around in his mouth to get a better taste of it.)

"An absolute disaster. Empty bottles, empty rooms. I am now forced to depend on this young man for absolutely everything. Aren't I, Gabriel? Absolutely everything.

"You could say, gentlemen, that I am placing myself entirely in his capable hands.

"And now, gentlemen, I would ask you all to rise, to raise the very last glass of champagne in the house, and to join me in a toast.

"Gentlemen, I give you, AN END TO ALL THIS."

And now the wineglass did get smashed; Mr Clive proposed his toast with a great sweeping gesture, only to have the glass fly out of his hand and shatter against a wall.

Nobody stood up; nobody even reached for their glass. The man who had told me he was a dancer choked on his champagne, let out a tiny high-pitched giggle and said, *oh dear, I think that's what they call bringing the house down.* One of the other guests snapped at him to please shut up. Mr Clive swayed where he stood for a moment and then sat down carefully and composed himself.

"And now, gentlemen, I am sure you would all agree that you had better leave. Please show yourselves out. There is nothing left. I assure you, there is nothing left to eat or drink or stare at in the entire house. Just go, please. You've seen it all, now go."

It was clear from his voice that if we didn't leave promptly then he was about to start shouting. Gabriel opened the dining-room doors and we all left. I don't remember anyone saying anything to anyone. I didn't even look at him, sitting there at the head of that ruined table, with Gabriel by his side. I was the last to go, and as I passed him, still sitting there and staring straight ahead as if his twin was still there, still sitting in the chair I'd just left, I thought I heard him say, very quietly, "Happy Birthday, Mr Page"; but I can't be sure. I left the dining-room and I went down the stairs and I went home; we all went home and left them there alone together, and I have never spoken to anyone about that evening, not ever.

I walked all the way home that night; I didn't want to get on a bus, the state I was in. The cold air was good for clearing my head. It wasn't so much what he had said, but the way he had threatened me with it, the way I was sure that for two pins he would have told everybody there that it was my birthday too, that he wasn't the only one who had the key to the door now. And I couldn't get the moment where he had grabbed Gabriel's wrist in that way out of my mind. I mean it wasn't as if this was a room full of old friends and even if it had been then I can't stand that sort of behaviour. Never could. Touching him in front of everyone like that. I saw two men do that a few weeks ago to the waiter with the forearms in the Italian place in Poland Street, practically flirting with him, in front of everybody, and one of them actually more or less stroked his arm, making out that he was just asking for another cup of coffee. Now I'm not saying that I

but I really find that sort of thing humiliating.

I walked home so fast that I must have been practically running.

That was the Saturday night. Another pot of tea, and then I'll do the Sunday morning and afternoon. If I can get that bit right then it's all done really, and I might not have the dream tonight, which would be good, seeing as how it's work tomorrow morning. Wish me luck darling.

Seven p.m. twenty-sixth.

I never wanted a bird, or a dog. I always had a radio though; it was one of the first things that I ever saved up for.

They say that birds can't help themselves from singing if you put them out in the sun; well, that Sunday, the fourteenth, it was a beautiful day, a really beautiful day. I stayed in until well past lunchtime, cleaning, which is what I do when I'm angry. Cleaning and scraping and thinking and thinking. Still trying to clear my head I was, still furious. And then by the time I found myself out and walking – walking, not strolling, very determined I was to get this out of my system – there was real warmth in the sun. First time that year we had felt that. I remember thinking oh he'll be able to turn that bloody heating off now. Walking past the window of the pet shop at the top of Camden High Street and stopping for a moment to stare at all the cock canaries going mad in the sunlight. All singing their tiny little bright yellow hearts out, with their hot little beaks wide open, demented – and you couldn't hear a single note because of the plate glass. I stayed there quite a while staring at them, bird-brains, brains smaller than a lizard, a whole chorus line of them hopping mad and singing their hearts out and all to no avail, no one could hear a single note of it. A bit like me really, having all these great shouting matches and confessions in my head and never uttering a word of any of them, walking along with my head raging and chattering and still making not a single squeak to disturb the silent Sunday streets with. I may have looked quiet, a young man out for a quiet walk on a Sunday, but if you could have heard what I was thinking – *stop asking me what I think you should do just bloody stop asking me all right? Stop looking at me like that in the middle of your speeches, just ask him, why don't you. You're worse than me, always hanging around and hinting at things. Why don't you just ask him? Why don't you just come right out and ask him.*

That was what I was going to say. Oh yes. Right up on my high horse I was. I was going to give him the real morning after speech. *You asked me for my advice and well now here it is,* that was the general gist. I was going to throw back those heavy dining-room curtains, let some sunlight in, get a good cup of proper strong tea down him and really speak my mind. I mean I was twenty-one myself that Sunday morning, and it wasn't as if I didn't know anything about anything, it wasn't as if I didn't have my own opinions. And what I was going to say to him was *Oh, if I was in your position Mr Clive; oh if I was in your situation, I wouldn't wait a day longer,* because you see Mr Clive there is nothing stopping you. Nobody to stop you doing it. Nobody can see you in there and nobody can hear you, and so you see, Mr Clive, you could do it; you've got him right there in your house already. The difficult thing is always asking them if they have somewhere to go, I find, and well, you'll never have to ask him that, so you could do it, Mr Clive, you could get away with it.

So what are you waiting for? No wonder I remember it all so well. I rehearsed that speech all the way from my flat to his house and believe me, I did a really good job of learning it by heart. Repeating it. Telling myself that I wasn't in his situation and I never was going to be in his situation. Telling myself very definitely that getting away with it was something that was always going to happen to other people but not to me. Telling myself that right across Camden Town on that morning of Sunday the fourteenth of March, right across Camden Town and all the way round Regents Park, the long way round, and all the way down to Oxford Circus and along to Duke Street and left down Duke Street and then left into Brooke Street. All the way while I walked along the dark side of the street and then stopped just across from number eighteen and got myself ready to cross over and ring the bell. I remember the incredible noise in my head, the blood and my speeches and that phrase over and over again, *what are you waiting for,* never *what was I waiting for,* but what was he waiting for, what are you waiting for, you, not me, *never me,* I never thought of doing it myself, *you*, what are *you* waiting for. All that noise.

Then everything going silent.

And now this isn't the dream. This is how it actually happened.

I looked up at the outside of the house. The stones were a beautiful dark red in that sunshine, more beautiful than I had ever seen them. Every single detail. Nobody can see you in there and nobody can hear you, I was thinking, not behind those great stone walls. Imagine being in that situation. The stones were red, and the roof was red, the sun was full on it; and I looked down to where the servants' rooms were, the staff bedrooms with their odd, bare windows that looked as if they are cut straight into the stone. And then down, to the next floor, and there in the sunlight, on the left, was the open window.

And there, of course, in the window, was Gabriel.

With nothing moving but the air – on his lips, and in his white hair. Under his arms, and between his legs. Standing there for the whole world to see, and nobody there to see him except me. Naked. Naked in a street in Mayfair, he really was. Naked. Naked in the kind of sunshine that you only ever get after a bad night, a really bad one.

He hadn't come out here to show himself to anyone, it wasn't a formal appearance on the balcony before the people or anything like that. He didn't know that anyone was watching him, and I think that perhaps he didn't even know that he was naked. Something had happened that had made him forget all that.

Every detail. I looked at every part of him. The flat base of his stomach, all of him. And this moment feels just the same now as it felt then; everything that I think, and everything that I have been so scared of, all those words, they just go right out of me. There are, and were, no sounds at all; no words, no footsteps, no traffic. All of last night and all of the rest of the city just goes, and there is just Gabriel, standing there, all of him, naked, with his white hair, letting the light soak into him. If anyone else had been there then of course to them the sight of him standing there like that would have been, well, ridiculous. Incomprehensible.

For them there would have been no possible reason why he should have been there; it was hardly the kind of thing one expects on a Sunday afternoon in that part of town or indeed any part. There would have been no reason for a young man to appear like that. But I knew why he was there. I knew as soon as I saw him. I knew, because although when Mr Clive showed me round the house he never got as far as showing me the bedrooms, he had told me where in the house the staff bedrooms were, and which floor his own bedroom was on. And so you see I knew which window that open window, the one on the left, was. I knew that Gabriel hadn't just got out of his own bed.

And when, after a long, silent minute (it can have only been a minute, though I keep on thinking that it was much longer), Gabriel smiled, I knew that it was at the sound of someone inside the house saying his name. And then, when he turned to look over his shoulder, I knew just who he was turning to see.

And that's when I couldn't bear it of course. That's when I had to look down and pretend to be looking at my watch. Blood everywhere. Because you see up until that moment I really had tried to tell myself that Mr Clive was like me, that he was always waiting, always looking, but never

never taking them back to his house.

never having a man spend the night in your room, in your bed, and still being there in the morning, and still being there in the afternoon, oh god, still being there, still being there a whole week later.

And so I looked away, I looked down, I had to, because it was two o'clock on an early March afternoon. Two o'clock on the early afternoon of March the fourteenth. 1924.

And as I said, when I looked back up, he had gone. So I crossed the street. To climb the steps. To ring the bell. To open the door. To climb the stairs.

I am stopping for a moment just now and pouring myself the tea. There is no milk left. It is quite dark, as dark as three in the morning, although it is still only just gone twenty-past seven.

There is no one at all moving outside, nothing at all to interrupt me or prevent me. The snow stops everything, doesn't it, fixes everything. "Quite still" is the phrase it always makes me think of. I am noting the weather and the time exactly like this because I want everything to be exact now. I want this next part to come back exactly.

Now that it has happened and is all in the past, I don't ever want to look away again or look down, not ever.

·············

When the next part happened, it didn't happen exactly as it happens in the dream. For instance, of course I went up the steps to get to the front door, but I didn't *climb* them; that is only how it feels in the dream. In the dream, it feels like I am climbing the steps to a castle, to something important. To the great armoured door of a castle. But actually all I did was walk up the steps to the front door of a house I'd already been in several times.

And when I reached the door, it wasn't unlocked, like it is in the dream. It was very firmly locked. Too bloody right. Too bloody right they've got the door locked is what I thought. Blood everywhere, I shouldn't wonder.

I rang the bell. Several times. And nobody came. I kept on ringing. I was imagining the scene upstairs, the panic, the whispers, Mr Clive trying to find his trousers (and he was always so proud of the way he dressed; now I'd caught him out), wondering who the hell that could be, wondering had they really locked the door, sending the boy running naked down the corridor and up the stairs to his own room. Oh no, he certainly wasn't expecting me this time. Hastily brushing down his hair so that I wouldn't see that somebody had been running their hands through it, grabbing it and pulling him down.

Still no one came, but I just kept on ringing. I wonder what I would have done if they simply hadn't answered? Would I have gone out into the middle of Brooke Street and shouted up at the front of the house, shouted I KNOW YOU'RE IN THERE, kept on shouting until they would have had to let me in just to stop the racket?

Yes, I think I might even have done that. Mr Page was hardly himself that afternoon.

My hand was still on the bell when the door opened. It was Gabriel.

It wasn't him I was expecting; it wasn't him I had prepared my speech for.

He was wearing the dark blue jacket from the night before, and for a moment I thought he was fully dressed. That stopped me in my tracks; I just stood there like an idiot, staring at him. You see I couldn't work out how he could have possibly had time to have got dressed in the time it had taken me to cross the street and ring the bell. And then (typical of me), my first thought was that I must have just *imagined* seeing him naked in the window, barely a minute earlier – imagined seeing him like that because that was how I wanted to see him. And that I'd got it all wrong and that what I thought was going on in that house was in fact just going on inside my dirty, chattering mind. But then I saw that the top three buttons of the jacket were undone, and that he had no shirt underneath. And no underwear either beneath the black trousers I suppose (I told you, I notice these things). I couldn't look him in the face, because of that, I had to look down – and he wasn't wearing any shoes. He had come to the door barefoot. So I knew. I hadn't imagined it.

And that wasn't all that was wrong. One of the pair of bronze vases that stood in the hall fireplace was lying on its side, and one of the gold plates was in splinters on the floor behind him. On the stairs, I could see what looked like torn clothing, a shirt or something.

What on earth would they have done if it hadn't been me that was ringing the bell that afternoon, if it hadn't have been me who'd seen the hallway in that state? What on earth would Gabriel have said or done, coming to the door looking like that, if it had been a stranger? Or was he so ignorant of what was meant to happen and what was not meant to happen that he thought there wasn't a problem answering the door all unbuttoned like that and half of London knowing there was nobody but the two of them in the house that afternoon?

But it wasn't a stranger, it was me; and Gabriel knew who I was. He looked at me very calmly, very collected for somebody who had been naked in another man's bedroom just a minute earlier, and he didn't do any of the things that a servant should do. He didn't offer to take my coat and ask me to come in or ask me what I wanted or would I please wait here. He just looked straight at me, and he smiled.

He knew who I was, you see. He knew I was the man who had sat opposite his master the night before and had never said a word.

He turned his back on me and left me standing there in the doorway while he crossed the hall and pushed a staff bell – one I hadn't noticed before, concealed in the panelling just under the mantel of the fireplace. He didn't seem to care what I thought, and he didn't seem to be worried about cutting his feet on the pieces of broken glass either. Perhaps we were all still slightly drunk, I don't know. Sometimes it's just like that, after

after you get out of bed.

After he'd rung the bell Gabriel turned round to watch my face, to see my reaction. I knew Mr Clive had said that there were no other servants left at number eighteen, that they had all left because of the money, but when I saw Gabriel ringing the bell, I don't know why – perhaps because of the way he was smiling, the way he definitely looked like he knew something that I didn't – but I took a step back towards the doorway, because I thought that that butler or whatever who had been there the first time I had ever gone to the house was going to reappear; that in the middle of all this he was going to appear looking very proper in his black coat and behaving as if this was all completely normal; and that he was going to come right up to me while Gabriel just stood there unbuttoned and practically grinning at me and say to me, *Yes sir and how can I help you? What exactly was it that you wanted? Mr Page, isn't it?*

But of course it was Mr Clive that Gabriel was ringing for; it was Mr Clive who answered the summons. It was the master who came when the servant called, it was Mr Clive who appeared at the top of the stairs wearing only the grey silk dressing-gown with the lemon yellow piping, Mr Clive who came slowly down the stairs of number eighteen Brooke Street towards me, staring at me standing there in the doorway and not saying a word and not having to, because he was making the situation quite clear with every step that he took; *you see, Mr Page, when this boy rings, I come. He doesn't even have to use my name or look to see if it's me; I come. And I don't care who knows it.* And as he came down the stairs, treading on the torn evening clothes that lay strewn on the steps, the dressing-gown fell open, and I could see that he wasn't wearing anything underneath. I suppose he didn't need to, what with that heating, and the sunshine. I could see that his chest was bruised, and that

the hair on his head was stiff, unbrushed, and the hair on his stomach was

I mean you could see exactly what they had been doing. Like flakes of glue, on his stomach.

And because of the heat I could smell him. He hadn't washed himself. And sweat, and brandy – there was brandy spilt down the front of the dressing-gown. Sweat and brandy and all the rest. He stood there on the bottom step and let me look at him, or made me look at him; at the bruises on his chest, at the small cut on his forehead, teeth- or nail-marks on the side of his neck, and that expression in his eyes, *you know exactly why I look like this, don't you, Mr Page, we can take that for granted, but what I really want you to see is that I don't care, I don't care Mr Page. I've got the key to the door and when you went home last night we used the key to lock the door from the inside.* Oh god – oh god I can see him now. I can see him now taking the final step and walking across the hall and standing just behind Gabriel with the light from the open front door behind me falling on them, standing together, and falling on the rose marble of the fireplace. I can see why I kept on going back to the house, and I can see why I keep on going back even now, in the dream I mean. Because when the grey silk dressing-gown fell open I saw all over again that it could have been me. It could have been me standing there. It was my own body that I was seeing there with the bruises and the teeth-marks and the hair all stuck to his stomach. My own neck bitten and my own chest bruised and the hair on my own stomach matted like that. It was me standing there half naked in the daylight, bitten and stained and smiling and not having to explain anything, just as surely as it was me standing on the other side of the hall with my back to the light buttoned up and blushing and needing an explanation to almost everything.

And then Mr Clive laughed at me.

He laughed at me. And now when I remember it that laugh of his sounds like myself laughing at myself, an awful, easy laugh, which is a terrible thing to hear after all these years.

And still laughing he put a hand on Gabriel's shoulder and said, "Well," he said, "Mr Page. And what can we do for you?"

He gave just a slight emphasis to that word *we*, he made quite sure that I'd heard it, quite sure that I saw his hand on Gabriel's shoulder like that. His voice was hoarse, but very strong, not exhausted at all. The two of them were like dogs, mastiffs, two dogs used to working as a pair, standing there in the hallway of their house, very relaxed, but ready to jump if anyone raised their voice or made the wrong move. The way a big dog looks at you and begins to growl the moment before its hackles go up.

I hesitated – I was always hesitating in those days. I blame myself for that now – and Mr Clive didn't give me a chance. The dog made its move; just a slight raising of the voice, the equivalent of the beginning of that low growling that tells you that you have to make up your mind to leave now.

"I would invite you in for some breakfast or something but as you can see . . . as you can see I'm down to the absolute minimum of staff.

"I'm sure you understand, Page."

I tried to talk to him, I really did. I tried to stand up to him. A second later and I think I would have found my voice, I would have said LOOK I HAVE TO TALK TO YOU. I HAVE TO TALK TO YOU ABOUT LAST NIGHT, ABOUT but Mr Clive couldn't wait that long; his voice suddenly snapped, and turned into the voice of an angry customer – the way they talk to you if you query a payment or tell them there will be a delay in delivery –

"And the fact is, Page, I have just got up. In fact you have just got me up, ringing that bloody bell, and quite frankly I hadn't intended getting out of bed for several hours, if you get my drift. Which I'm sure you do, Page, I'm sure – "

and here his voice changed or changes, I should say, because I am actually hearing it now, his voices changes again, he knows he has won, he knows he can be kind to me.

" – I am sure that you understand."

Mr Clive comes up to me now and he puts one hand on each of my shoulders and there we are standing face to face and eye to eye again, in the middle of the hallway of number eighteen, in the middle of Mayfair, in the spring – and the door is wide open, anyone could walk by and see us, anyone. And there's something in his voice now that I never heard at any other time. He is sorry for me. I know that; he is sorry for me because of what he has and I don't, and also in some way he is telling me that he needs me, that I was – that I was of some use in this story.

"Why don't you come back tomorrow morning. If you come back then, I promise I'll be up, and we can talk. Gabriel here can do almost everything for me that I need done but there is one thing that he can't do, which is listen and understand every word I say. And I meant what I said in the Square, Mr Page; I do need somebody to talk to about this. And I meant what I said last night; this is the end. The absolute, living end. Could you call in on your way to work?"

That was the only time I was absolutely sure that he wasn't lying to me. It was the only time he ever talked to me like that. And it was also the last time that he ever talked to me.

··············

Bodies are especially hard things to lift or carry. A man's body is a very heavy thing to lift, it is a very hard kind of secret to carry around all day, on the bus, in the lift, especially when the lift is so crowded first thing in the morning. And then at the end of the week or on Saturday afternoon or at night, it's hard to get it up the stairs without bumping into the walls and making all sorts of noise. On the other hand, having a secret that you know you must never share makes you very good at all that. I mean in my case I don't think anyone has ever known that I was humping all that around with me, backwards and forwards from work every day just a few streets away from where it all happened. I do it very well. I'm a real dab hand when it comes to tucking things away, a real back-of-the-drawer artist. Because you never know when you might need it, your secret. Never know when it's going to come in handy. Never know when you're going to be stuck in the flat for four days and be glad that you've got something tucked away at the back of the cupboard. Something no one else would have found even if they'd looked. Even if they had gone through this place with a toothcomb. Oh no, because I made a lovely job of it; all wrapped up and tucked away and I should think it's been thirty years now since I got it out and had a really good look at it. Because you see it wasn't just a secret, was it Mr Page? Oh no. It was a crime. It doesn't matter how beautiful he was, that's not the point; it was a crime. Because you see we were never friends, Mr Clive and I, never that, we were something much stronger than friends. We were partners in crime. From the moment I caught him watching me in Jermyn Street to that very last moment when he said that he needed someone to talk to we were like that. We both knew (though we never said it to each other, not in so many words) that only two things matter in life, really. Having a secret, and keeping a secret. Which is to say, doing it, and getting away with it.

I may have tried to tell myself many times since that afternoon that life's not really like that; I see the young men these days, and I read the papers, and believe you me, I have on many occasions tried to talk myself out of feeling like this. Because I know that this is not like other crimes. There are no trunks or cupboards or wallpaper or floorboards. There are no hands taped together and there is none of that awful business that you read about of having to cut quickly and efficiently at the neck in order to stop the screaming. But the body is still there, and there are all the usual criminal precautions to be taken; the locked doors, the muffling of sounds so that the neighbours won't hear. And if the two people involved in the secret or crime meet accidentally then they have to pretend that they have never met. And lies have to be told that are so clever and so convincing that not even close colleagues in the same Department, never mind neighbours, suspect, even though it's been going on for years. Not even Mrs Welch downstairs suspects, for instance. But in the end (and this is the real similarity between the secret and the crime) in the end, just like in all the worst cases that you've ever read about, what it all comes down to in the end, and what will finally lead to you being caught, is the fact that there is a body. Not a slip of the tongue or a sum of money or a slip of paper. A body.

And the thing is, if you have been party to a crime and then they never do catch you, if you never are interrogated, if you never do see the details of your case written up in all the papers, not even on page five, and if you have had to carry it all around for thirty odd years or to keep it all in the back of the cupboard, well then when you do finally have to make your statement it can be very hard to get the details right. To get your evidence right. The details.

Which is why in the dream it gets all mixed up.

It starts right enough, but then it gets all mixed up.

I confuse it with what happened later.

Because as I said what actually happened was that I rang and rang and then Gabriel answered the door; but in the dream I ring and ring and I ring, but nobody comes. And then I reach out my hand and I discover that the door is unlocked. It's been left unlocked. It swings open. I go up the stairs to the bedroom. I stand in the doorway. And. And I know I'm going to see what is on the bed, and I do. And his eyes are closed and his hair is white. And then I can't look and I have to look down. Blood everywhere. And then I call out to him, his lover calls out to him, he calls out his name, but he doesn't look over his shoulder or smile. He doesn't move. How odd.

Eight p.m. twenty-sixth.

Oh shit, oh dear, brandy everywhere. Brandy right down the front of my gown. Half naked with the gas on full and my glass half empty and no wonder my bloody wrist hurts well did you think I don't do it any more just because I'm over fifty. "Helplessly drunk", that's what people say, isn't it, well; *helpfully drunk* would be more like it. Not that I would want anybody to think that I couldn't do this without. Eight o'clock on a Boxing Day evening, it makes me want to laugh. Because all over London at this time people are getting helpfully drunk. This is the time when everybody feels that the festivities have been going on just that little bit too long, of course it was lovely that Anne managed to make it down from Watford, but the children are getting just a little too loud. Over-tired I expect; you know how it is. Time to be thinking about that train home really. Time for one last one before going. And all over London people are about to speak their minds to their nearest and dearest, it is that distinctive eight o'clock and one too many feeling, just the one more and certain people are going to be obliged to say just exactly what they are feeling. What they are actually thinking about. As Mr Clive put it so succinctly on that now-distant occasion *I am sure you understand, Mr Page* and indeed I do. Indeed I do understand and I do know what I am actually thinking.

Indeed I did know what was going on.

And so now I have had my drink I think I am ready to make my statement, your Honour. I am ready to tell you "in graphic detail", as they always say, what it's like when somebody has to wait and wait and wait for something and then finally they can't be polite any longer.

Yes, your Honour, that is correct.

Yes I did go home on that Saturday night, I did hear the door of number eighteen close behind me and I think you are correct to assume that it was then locked but nevertheless, your Honour, I can just see it. I can just see what happened next inside the house.

Because I know exactly how it feels, your Honour.

I want to make my statement, your Honour. I am speaking up, thank you, your Honour. I said, *I Want to Make a Full Statement.*

Thank you, your Honour.

MR PAGE'S STATEMENT

When I arrived at number eighteen Brooke Street it was seven-thirty exactly. I am quite sure of the time because punctuality has always been one of my strong points. I rang the door bell several times. It was not the manservant who opened the door but Mr Clive. He seemed to be quite nervous. I noticed that his shirt cuff was soiled and that his hair was untidy which was not like him.

At the time I thought this was all a bit odd.

On entering the house I was led straight to the front parlour and thence directly to the dining-room. This was very different to my previous visit to the house when Mr Clive had been very eager to show me round the whole place. It was at this point in the evening that I began to conjecture that some effort was being made to conceal the true state of affairs in the house from the guests.

The dining-room was done up magnificently. I had never seen anything like it. Mr Clive had told me that all the other staff in the house had left prior to the evening of the thirteenth and so I was wondering how just the two of them could have done all this by themselves. Obviously it was a very important occasion for Mr Clive being not only his birthday but also the day when he was going to come into his money. I don't think it can have been easy for him laying on a spread like that for eight people with no cook or housekeeper. Personally I think that it must mostly have been ordered over the phone since the manservant could not have done the shopping in person owing to his lack of English and Mr Clive would not I think have wanted to leave him alone in the house while he did it himself. Not to mention that that would hardly have been proper or have given a good impression if he had been seen shopping for himself. It was a very odd meal for a cold March evening I thought. I had the impression that it had been a very difficult day for Mr Clive. I think because of it being his twenty-first he must have been brooding on the fact that he was now alone in the house with no parents or legal guardians. He certainly gave the impression of a man deep in thought. I know speaking for myself that I was also on that day thinking of the effects and consequences of being twenty-one, of being one's own master so to speak. I think that by half-past seven the tension must have been considerable.

At seven twenty-five Mr Clive had only just begun to dress himself for the evening and was therefore in a hurry. When he heard the doorbell ring he assumed that Gabriel would get it, but when he heard the bell go a second time he realised that Gabriel was otherwise occupied and went to get it himself. As he made his way downstairs he encountered Gabriel on the stairs, also hurrying in order to get changed before the first guest arrived. They passed on the stairs, which is always unlucky. As they did so they almost collided and Mr Clive had occasion to grab the boy by the arm. Without thinking Gabriel put his hand up into Mr Clive's hair, and then before they knew where they were they were kissing. At the same time they could still hear the ringing of the doorbell.

I do not know if this was the first time such an incident had occurred.

They then broke apart and Gabriel proceeded up the stairs to change. Mr Clive opened the front door with his hair still disarranged. He did not at any time mention to me or to any of the guests what had occurred on the stairs. All of the other guests were gentlemen. I had the definite impression on several occasions during the meal that Mr Clive wished to touch Gabriel. I now realise that having worked so hard to prepare for this meal he in fact spent the whole evening wishing that it was over and that we would all go home so that he could find out what was going to happen next.

During the meal Mr Clive made a long speech which was meant to be about the house and him coming into his inheritance but was in fact mostly about older men getting on trains or throwing themselves under them and how he knew just how they felt on account of the papers these days. I think Mr Clive had realised at seven-thirty that evening that there was now no point in him pretending that any of that mattered any more, not to a man in his situation.

He then asked us would we all please collect our own coats and would we please leave now.

I was the last guest to leave. Gabriel followed me downstairs and he closed the front door behind me and locked it. I imagine that he must have been wondering what was going to happen now, was he going to lose his job and so on. Was the master of the house going to kiss him again or had that just been a sudden loss of control.

Presumably he must have been aware of the conspicuous manner in which Mr Clive had been staring at him and had also presumably understood some of his after-dinner speech despite his lack of perfect command of the English language. He closed the front door, and then he felt the breath on the back of his neck. As I say I do not think that during the meal he knew what was going to happen, but at this point he certainly must have realised. When he felt the breath on the back of his neck like that, and when he realised how deliberately and how quietly Mr Clive had followed him downstairs and come up behind him. How Mr Clive couldn't wait a minute longer now that the door was locked. Gabriel attempted to turn round, presumably in order to say something, but Mr Clive very quickly had him pinned against the door. He is very strong, Mr Clive. He has got arms like mine. It is also true I think that being drunk can make you stronger than you actually are.

Gabriel twisted and kicked and also banged hard against the front door, however by this time I had walked down the steps and turned on to Brooke Street, which was why I did not hear any of this happening. Why I did not hear the noise of his body being thrown up against the door.

He eventually managed to get Mr Clive off his back and to push him away across the hallway. Mr Clive staggered on the polished hall floor, and this is the point at which the brass vase in the fireplace was kicked over. They then stared at each other for a moment across the hall, Gabriel with his back to the door. Then, *then I could have them calm down I suppose. Or I could have them just fall into each other's arms and that's all we'd really see. But that isn't how I imagine it at all. Because you don't go through all of that waiting and waiting and then just fall into each other's arms and it's all lovely, that isn't how it works, your Honour. I know that isn't how it works, believe me. And nobody really knew how things were in that house but I think I knew more than most so you'll just have to take my word for it dear. Your Honour.* Then they just stand there for a bit, heaving and staring at each other across the hall like two wrestlers who are pondering their next move. Then Gabriel makes his; he collects himself, he crosses the hall and heads for the stairs. He has decided that he is going to go upstairs and start clearing up and so on and then just see how things feel in the morning. But our Mr Clive can't wait that long. Oh no, he can't wait, he's waited quite long enough. And our Mr Page knows just how he feels. He knows how it feels when the time comes quite suddenly when you can't wait any longer.

Mr Clive moves as fast as a cat after a bird; he catches Gabriel on the fourth step of the stairs, and straight away he's got him down in a clumsy kind of flying tackle. As Gabriel goes down he cuts his forehead open on one of the steps, or at least grazes it badly enough for there to be blood. He tries to get up the stairs, but he's being pulled down by Mr Clive, who's got him by the right ankle. Gabriel grabs on to the banister to try and haul himself up. But the Master won't let him go, he's not going to let him get away this time, not now.

Gabriel has managed to twist himself over on to his back. The stairs are cutting into the small of his back; he is holding on to the banister with one hand to stop himself from being pulled down again, and he is kicking out viciously with his free foot, trying to break Mr Clive's grip on his ankle, kicking out as hard as he can. The whole thing is being done in complete silence. All you can hear are the sounds of desperate breathing and of cloth beginning to tear. Mr Clive takes one of Gabriel's kicks full on the chest, but he manages to avoid getting it in the face. Then he suddenly lets go, and again he makes his move before the boy is expecting it or can get away; now Mr Clive is up on top of him, he has got him face down again, he has got his left arm hooked around Gabriel's throat and with his right hand he is prising Gabriel's fingers off the banister, trying to break his grip by bending his fingers right back. Gabriel's face is being pushed into the stair carpet, the spit from his open mouth and the blood from his grazed forehead are being ground into the pattern of the carpet. Mr Clive is biting and kissing the back of his neck now, and now he is using his right hand to tear at Gabriel's high silver-buttoned collar, he yanks at it until the boy is half-choked but then the buttons burst off and now Mr Clive can get at that neck. He is biting and kissing it, and Gabriel is burying his face in the carpet, twisting and turning to avoid those teeth, so that Mr Clive can't get at the lips and cheeks that he wants so much to fill his mouth with, he can't get at the tears which Gabriel is crying now and which Mr Clive wants so badly to taste. Gabriel still has his grip on the banister, and now he gets the other hand free too, and using the banister and the banister rails (it isn't easy, his hands slip on the polished wood) he is hauling himself slowly but surely up the stairs, dragging both himself and the man who is clinging to his back up towards the first landing, step by step. Mr Clive sounds as though he is sobbing now too; that can happen when you're drunk. He collapses on Gabriel's back, with his arm still locked around the boy's neck, and in that position he holds on, like an exhausted boxer will hold on to his opponent; he lets himself become exhausted and defeated, all his energy goes out of him. Now Gabriel gets half up on his knees, with the Master still clinging to his back, and he uses both hands on the banister, hand over hand as if he was pulling on a rope, and that way he manages to haul both himself and his burden up the first flight of stairs and on to the first landing.

They fall together on to the landing. It's as if Gabriel had just brought someone up out of a mine, just hauled an injured man out of the rubble and up a ladder to safety. Or out from under ice – or from the twisted wreckage of the boiler room of a sinking liner – you know, any of the times that the captain clings to the soldier for dear life, and they both draw those great, ragged, tearing breaths as if their chests would split. They fall apart now that the immediate danger is over; Mr Clive lets go and rolls away from Gabriel (now I've got it; it's as if he had just been hauled up a cliff, inch by sweating inch, and now, at last, exhausted, they can haul themselves up over the edge of the cliff and throw themselves panting on to the flat rocks of safety); he lies on his back with one arm thrown over his face and his knees pointing at the ceiling. His lip is split. Neither of them is looking at the other. Gabriel puts a hand up to his forehead to see how badly he is bleeding, and then he gets himself up off the carpet, he is about to stand and make his way up the rest of the stairs to his room, but he is still a bit shocked, a bit slow, and in the time it takes him to get his bearings and to steady himself Mr Clive sees him, and his strength returns; he is up on his feet and he grabs Gabriel by one shoulder and spins him round.

I've got them face to face now, I could have them kiss if I wanted to, split lips and all

But that's not what I see. That's not how it was.

That's not how it was.

Mr Clive wants Gabriel to understand how he is feeling after having been made to wait for so long, and he can't help himself. Someone has made him wait, somebody must be to blame, somebody has to feel what he is feeling; and so he hits Gabriel across the face. Left, right, left, right, with the full force of the front or back of his hand each time, four full ringing slaps that nearly knock the young man over. Somebody had to be hit, and Gabriel's is the nearest face. He takes each blow full across the face, two on each side, and each one makes his face turn and his hair fly. And of course he starts to cry again – it's a natural reaction to being hit like that. Like a child or a boy would cry. And now there is the first real kiss between them, because that is part of Mr Clive needing the young man to feel what he is feeling, too; the first real, proper, deliberate kiss between them. Mr Clive has the taste of the other man's tears now, and now I think for the first time in his life Gabriel has the amazing sensation of another man's tongue in his mouth. They stand there on the landing and they kiss; Mr Clive takes Gabriel's face in both hands and kisses him and kisses and kisses him and it has never been like this before for either of them, not like this, not ever.

No your Honour I am not making this up.

I am fully aware that I am under oath here.

If I was making it up then how would I know how it feels your Honour?

And now Gabriel is kissing him back.

And now they part for a moment, and Gabriel sets to work on his master's clothes. He knows every detail of these clothes, from all the times that he has laid them out on the bed ready for Mr Clive. He knows precisely how they all hang, button and fold. He takes off Mr Clive's dinner jacket in two swift, well-practised moves. Then he stoops to remove the sapphire links from the dress-shirt cuffs. Mr Clive makes no attempt to stop him and does not ask for any explanation. Gabriel certainly seems to know what he is doing – maybe he worked as a valet once before; or maybe he trained as a tailor. He certainly works as if he was a tailor, as if he was working at a dummy, draping and cutting, his mouth full of pins and his brow furrowed with concentration – exactly the way that you see them cutting and pinning and tucking in Jermyn Street or in our own Menswear Department. He kneels, and unlaces and then removes the shoes, then the socks. He's working fast now. As each garment is removed, he doesn't fold it neatly, or pass it to an assistant; he simply drops it, or sometimes even flings it away. These clothes will never be needed again seems to be his assumption. One shoe strikes and shatters one of the glass plates; the dinner jacket ends up draped over the banister. The two men are so intent on what is happening that neither of them notices the havoc they are causing. Gabriel's hands are moving with great speed but no haste; it is all very methodical. Garment by garment. When he has got Mr Clive standing there in just his shirt and his underwear Gabriel seems not to be content to simply remove his clothing. As if he also had something to say, as if he too wanted the other man to know something of what he is feeling, he begins to tear. The seams of a hand-made Jermyn Street shirt are hard to tear; but Gabriel manages it. He uses his teeth if he has to. He doesn't just want this man undressed; he wants him naked. He wants there never to be anything between them again, not a single stitch to keep their skins apart. When he gets the first sleeve off the shirt, he uses it to wipe the blood from his forehead, and then throws it aside as if it was a rag. Which it now is. Still there are no words at all; nothing is said. Nobody asks what the hell do you think you are doing or what the hell are you looking at. Nobody says What Are You Two Up To? The whole house is completely silent except for the sounds of Gabriel working; the light from the golden lilies is reflected in all the glass and the tiles, and it draws a heavy golden line along the side of the Japanese copper vase now lying in the marble fireplace; and on the magnificent turkey carpet that covers the polished wood of the first landing the Master of the House is being stripped by his Servant, and as his clothes come off, his skin is golden too. The light draws a thick, gold line across Master Clive's shoulders and along the muscles at the top of his arms, which are lightly shining with sweat. This great and beautiful and silent house, this house in which every single thing was chosen and arranged with such care, is now acquiring a new and beautiful decorative feature.

Number Eighteen will never be the same, will it? There are clothes everywhere, almost invisible stains of blood and tears on the stair carpet, a sapphire cufflink lost. No amount of cleaning will ever fully restore the house to its former condition. You could scrub and scrub and scrub and try and forget but the house will never be the same again. Once things like that have happened on your carpet your room never seems the same again; you turn on the light when you get home from work and look down and you can hear the noises and smell it and feel it and it all comes back –

When Gabriel has finally got him naked, he leads his Mr Clive across the landing and into the dining-room. From the debris on the table Gabriel takes one of the gold finger-bowls and the cleanest of the linen napkins, also the tall, thin-necked cut-glass jug of pale green oil from the cruet, and he puts these three things safely on the sideboard. He removes his gloves, dropping them on the floor. Now you can see that he is wearing a heavy golden ring; it is a family ring, Mr Clive's family ring – that's why it wasn't on his finger. He has given it to the boy on the very day that it became his to give. And I suppose it is all right for Gabriel to take off his gloves now that all the guests have gone and there is no one to see that he is wearing this ring. No one except me.

He goes back to the table, and then, without smiling, without hesitating (he is doing all this as if it was a job that needed doing – a job worth doing), he reaches right across the table and takes hold of the heavy damask tablecloth and then, turning his hand so that the seal in the signet ring is pressed into the wood through the cloth and leaves a deep groove across its polished surface, he slowly, deliberately pulls the cloth and everything on it towards him, and past him, so that it is all dragged on to the floor. He looks so like a matador when he does that that I'll swear on oath I can see sand spread on the dining-room floor to soak up the blood, I can see Mr Clive lowering his head so that his neck is ready for the sword to go in, I can hear him bellow. Gabriel completes the gesture by letting the cloth fall. Everything that had been so carefully washed and polished and laid out according to the book now lies in ruins at his feet. The candles scorch the tablecloth as they gutter and fall, only to be extinguished by the spreading stains of wine. The stems of the wine-glasses snap; one of them is struck across the bowl by the handle of a gold-plated knife and shivers into a mess of splinters, spiking the scarlet carcass of a split lobster as it slides from a gilt serving dish.

The house is soundproofed, remember; no one in the street can hear this devastation. The curtains are drawn, and there is no one there to stop them from doing this or to tell them that they shouldn't.

Having cleared the table, Gabriel now uses the rose-water from the finger-bowl and the linen napkin to wash Mr Clive. He washes him as if he was a child, standing in front of a gas fire; roughly, efficiently, quickly, making sure that he gets under his arms and behind his ears and between his legs with the napkin. When he throws it away, it is dirty. Then he takes the flask of oil and slowly, carefully dribbles a stream of it across the top of Mr Clive's shoulders and across the top of his chest, using precisely the right amount so that the oil runs the whole length of his body, runs down over all of him. Then he follows each trail of oil with the palms of his hands until every part of that man is shining, *every part do you hear me*

Now do you see that I know what I am talking about your Honour?

Now do you believe me that I'm not making this up not a word of it

Then Gabriel lays Mr Clive face down on the great bare mahogany table, the wood of which is warm to the touch, and he works on and he kneads and he strokes that body until it doesn't belong to Mr Clive any more, it surrenders. Every part of it is open.

When all the oil is worked into the skin they go upstairs, leaving all the lights in the house still burning. And it is not to Gabriel's room that they go, but to Mr Clive's room, the master bedroom, and there Gabriel lays Mr Clive down on the beautiful, expensive linen of what was once the family bed. Mr Clive reaches up into Gabriel's hair, not to pull him down or to force him, but just for the pleasure of seeing his own hand resting at last in that strange white hair. Still nothing has been said, and indeed Mr Clive doesn't know what to say; but he agrees to everything. And now the real shame begins; the words and whispers of one syllable begin to be heard, the words that sound almost the same in both their languages, *yes, no, christ*. Later in the night Mr Clive finds all of his voice, and every time that his face is pushed down into the white sheets by the weight of the man who is on top of him he says *Gabriel, Gabriel, Gabriel,* once with each heavy slow thrust, as if to prove to himself that this is actually happening, *Gabriel, Gabriel, Gabriel, Gabriel.*

Mr Page
8.45 p.m. December 26 1956
in the presence of Officer J. Maguire

done it now haven't I? Put my name to it. Imagine if somebody read that

··············

And now I expect you would like that cup of tea after all that wouldn't you Mr Page?

Well I don't mind if I do Officer, thank you.

That's quite all right, sir, my pleasure, although I'm afraid that we shall be keeping you just a little while longer. Sugar?

How long do you think it will take, Officer?

As long as it takes, I should say, Mr Page. (*He's looking back over what I said now. Oh it's very funny to see all that in somebody else's handwriting. That is how they do it, isn't it? They make you say it all out loud in your own words and then one of them copies it all down and you have to sign it at the end.*)

Now may I take it sir that this is the whole, and nothing but? I only ask sir because we do get confessions like this quite often you see sir and half the time they turn out to be pure – well, fabrication – fantasies I suppose we should call them. Copied out of novels purchased discreetly on the Charing Cross Road for the most part. Wartime friendships, schoolday reminiscences, that sort of thing. And then of course recently we've been getting a lot of the classical stuff, Scenes from a Roman Bath-house and so on, "Costume Drama", as they say, although lack of costume rather seems to be the point as far as I can tell. Now, to return to your own efforts sir. I mean this is hardly the sort of thing that is going to stand up in court, is it sir, to be quite frank with you. Hardly the sort of thing we can accept in a supposedly factual statement. Torn clothing and oil and faces pressed into pillows and so on.

But Officer it had to all come out eventually. It had to come out somewhere after all these years. And as you know I had had a few drinks it being Christmas, and I was on my own. And you know how it can be when you're up on the fifth floor and there's not a sound to be heard and it's been four days since you talked to a living soul and the snow has all settled and there's no one to stop you or interrupt or prevent you, well is it surprising that you start saying things out loud? Though of course I am fully aware that certain things should not be said out loud under any circumstances whatsoever, Officer, certain scenes are conducted in silence and quite right too, they hardly being suitable for public consumption as you so rightly say, scenes that are only permitted under quite strictly observed regulations and in the steam room only and certainly never on a weekday, I should think not. Scenes such as those to be occasionally glimpsed in the London and Provincial Turkish Bath Company, 76 Jermyn Street, London W1.

Every single Saturday afternoon for thirty years from 1923 onwards, right up to last week.

Except for those missing months from 1952 to 1954 when he seems to have been otherwise occupied on his Saturday afternoons, months when as you have doubtless already surmised Officer such scenes took place here in this very room. In front of this very fire, Officer. Officer Maguire. Where the regulations concerning the wearing of towels are less strict, you might say. Except that no one could have seen a thing even if we had left the windows open, could they Officer, not up here on the fifth floor. It was all behind locked doors, the whole thing, believe you me; him standing there in front of the gas, standing over me. Shining. And then later the pink walls and the gold light and the white sheets; no one saw a thing, none of it, no one saw it but me. So, Officer, shall we have that cup of tea now? Don't mind me if I get undressed and lay out my clothes for tomorrow. Iron a shirt. I do that every Sunday night before going back to work. Making sure that I don't forget to hide the body, you might say. You can get the body out for a couple of hours in the steam room at Jermyn Street or up here in front of the gas in the evenings, that's fine, but you must always remember to hide it again before Monday morning, isn't that right Officer. All those dead bodies, hidden all over London, hundreds of them, people have no idea. Just think, Officer.

21 The Taxation at Bethlehem
Pieter Bruegel The Elder, active 1551, died 1569.
Panel (chestnut) 116 x 164.5 cm. Signed lower right. Cleaned
1977–8

The subject is taken from St Luke Ch.2, v.1–5. Joseph, carrying
his carpenter's tools, is seen leading the ass on which Mary,
heavily pregnant, is riding. On the left of the painting can be
seen the inn, identified by a wreath of holly, which features in
several of Bruegel's Flemish genre scenes (see No. 22). Its doorway is crowded with those who have come to pay their taxes; it
is clearly the Biblical inn at which there was "no room".

The subject was rarely treated in Flemish painting, and Hulin
de Loo has suggested that the scene has its origins in the performance of contemporary religious plays or "mysteries" such as that
depicted by Cornelis Massys (Berlin). No contemporary record of
the work exists, although it is possible that this is the painting
listed in the collection of Cardinal Feuville under the erroneous
title of *The Flight Into Egypt*. As Grosman (1897) notes, the city
depicted in the upper right-hand corner of the painting is based
closely on the actual city in which the artist was resident in
1566, Amsterdam. The painting is therefore likely to have been
completed some three years before the artist's death, and seems
to share both the palette and the atmospheric preoccupations of
Winter Landscape with Travellers and Trap (1565). Michel (1931)
has argued that this group of paintings was directly inspired by
the hardships of the severe European winter of 1564.

Bruegel depicts the Biblical scene as apparently taking place
on a contemporary Christmas Eve in a specifically contemporary

Brabant village. The red sun, dipping momentarily below a bank of cloud evidently heavy with snow, is about to set. The extreme realism of the scene is, however, charged with an extraordinary impression of gloom and uncertainty. The darkening sky, the tiny figures isolated from each other by expanses of dirtied snow, the leper in his draughty hut of wattle and daub – in sharp contrast to the blazing fire in the cheerful, crowded inn – all seem to remind the spectator of the hardships of life rather more than of the happiness promised by the imminent birth of the Saviour. In particular, the figures of the children unconcernedly skating on the ice in the lower foreground remind us that this scene is the immediate precursor to its successor both in Bruegel's work and in the Biblical narrative, the *Slaughter of the Innocents* (no.22), which Bruegel was to depict as taking place in the very same village.

Certain features of this imaginary yet precisely imagined world remain inexplicable. An unidentifiable species of bird – an oddity in the work of an artist who usually depicts the natural world with absolute accuracy – hovers high over the village; only a prolonged study of the composition reveals that this sinister, owl-like figure occupies the position usually reserved for the depiction of a dove (symbol of the Holy Ghost), directly above the head of the Virgin. The hooves of the Virgin's donkey seem to have left no marks in the snow, whereas all the other figures in the painting have left footprints which are recorded by the artist with extraordinary realism. Most remarkably, all of the figures in the painting seem to be deliberately ignoring its central event. As if to draw attention to this mystery, an abandoned waggon wheel, half buried in the snow, has been placed by Bruegel so that its hub marks the precise geometrical centre of the painting. It is an overlooked symbol of the passing of time, an inconsequential detail which provides the single, fixed point around which the painting literally revolves.

Hist: coll.van Colen de Bouchot, Anvers; coll Ed. Huysbrechts, Anvers; acquired at sale of that collection 1860. Exhibited Bruges 1902, Paris 1923, Paris 1935. Bibl: De Loo, Ghent 1902, R. van Bastelaer, Bruxelles, 1907; A.E. Bye, London, 1923; F. Grosman,

Pieter Bruegel, The Complete Paintings, London and New York 1956.

from *Real Lives; Flemish Paintings from the Beaux Arts, Brussels*, catalogue, National Gallery, London, 1979, pp.26–7.

Wednesday, Twenty-Seventh
of December

That's right; Mr Page is taking a day off work, can you believe it. Four days I said I'd need, well it's going to take me five, and that's that. Thirty odd years and five days.

It feels like a Monday morning even though it is a Wednesday. Because I never really sleep well on a Sunday, what with thinking about work, and last night I didn't sleep either. Thinking about whether I'd got it all down or not. Lay there for ages wondering if it would come back again.

I don't think I've ever done this, not ever. Sat here like this at five to nine with a second cup knowing full well they'll be opening the doors in five minutes and I should be there.

That Monday, the fifteenth of March, would have been their first morning together. The Sunday doesn't count, what with the night before going on so long and then me disturbing them. The first morning – I mean the first time that you wake up in your usual bed and at exactly your usual time but wake up knowing that everything is different because you are not alone – that first morning is the special one, isn't it?

What did Mr Clive do, I wonder, on that morning of the fifteenth? I was getting up and doing my exercises and putting on my ironed shirt and getting on the number twenty-nine and turning into Mr Page, Banking. Did he get up and start to clean? Or did he just lie there, not thinking at all, not imagining anything, not even the next hour, just wanting the moment of waking up to go on for as long as possible? Lying there hardly daring to breathe. Just telling yourself, *yes, it's true, you know it's true, because you can feel how heavy his head is on your arm*. Oh it is so special that first morning. Afterwards, you want to remember it very much. You even try and go back and work out the exact date – you have to do that, because of course at the time you aren't thinking *oh, I must remember this*. You have no idea that it is going to be the first of many mornings. If you knew that then it would be impossible to bear. You would feel too much. But later it is all right if you go back and fix that date in your mind so that it becomes a special day. That date becomes like a photograph you can keep in the wallet in your inside pocket wherever you go. You can get it out and look at it if ever you feel you are in danger of forgetting. You can say the date quietly under your breath, and you feel just as happy as if you had seen a photograph of his face.

It wasn't until the third or fourth time that I can remember thinking, quite suddenly, *oh, this is the start of something*. I didn't know, you see, that I was going to have to remember anything. That remembering was going to be all that I would have.

That Monday, their first morning, was the wrong morning for Mr Clive to have asked me to go round. Not a Monday morning; I should have known as soon as he asked me that I'd never go. On a Monday Mr Page's weekend had to stop. That was what Monday meant. The weekend was for cleaning and for Jermyn Street, but when I laid the clothes out on Sunday night and ironed my shirt all that was put away again. And so I didn't call round at number eighteen that Monday morning. I went to work. I had to. And I went straight there every morning for the next five mornings, hearing Mr Clive's voice saying that he needed to talk to me every time I got off the number twenty-nine at the Dominion and started off down Oxford Sreet, knowing full well that as I was nearing Gilbert Street that all I had to do was to turn left and I'd be there. And each day of the week I would be telling myself (especially at lunchtimes), don't go, even if it is just round the corner, that's enough, that's it, who does he think he is? Saying he needs somebody to talk to. He's had plenty of chances to talk, hasn't he? I never felt comfortable in that part of town anyway. Every lunchtime and every evening that week I was thinking about everything I had seen, and especially what I had seen and what I had felt at two o'clock on that afternoon of March the fourteenth.

And then it was Saturday, and it was time for my afternoon in Jermyn Street. And I walked all the way there on that Saturday, setting out at my usual time, quite sure that I was going to get to the London and Provincial at exactly the same time as I always did, and then as I got to the door I just walked straight on past it and down towards Mayfair. I couldn't tell you why. I walked right past all the windows full of shirts and brushes and right past the back door of Simpson's and right along to Brooke Street and then for the fifth and final time I walked up the steps and rang the doorbell and that was it, that was when it happened; the door swung open.

I think I knew that they had gone as soon as I stepped into the hall.

It was cold, you see. It wasn't just that the door had been left open; the heating had been turned off. The bronze vase was still on its side in the fireplace.

Because there was no one there I straight away wanted to go and take a look at all the rooms he had never shown me – it was like being shut in the changing room and realising that Mr Maguire has gone home, that you could do whatever you wanted. I've often wanted that to happen. I can remember exactly what I did first; I reached up to the high shelf in the hall and I took down one of the glass vases and looked at it. I had never been able to look at one close up – or by daylight – and I had always wanted to know what colour they actually were – how they did that trick of darkening and turning into mirrors when the lights came on, and then managed to shine, or glow, or glimmer, however you say it, even when the hall was in almost complete darkness. When I held it in my hands I was shocked by how light it was. It didn't seem possible. I felt like I had done the wrong thing as soon as I touched it. You can look at things like that, but never touch them. Never actually have them in your hands. And imagining buying something like that, picking one out and saying *yes, I'll have that, thank you*. Well I can't. It looked as though there was a thin layer of metal under the glass – gold leaf, probably, I thought. But when I held it up against the light coming in through the open front door it was suddenly red, and tinged with purple, and transparent. An ear, with the sun behind it. The thin, half-dried slices of Italian ham on their silver plate at the café on Poland Street. The colour of blood when you cut your finger and run it under the tap. Not dark, like people expect it to be, but clear, vivid. So what I had always thought was made of gold, wasn't; I looked closer, and it was

that's wrong, I'm getting it wrong. I can see it, I can see it there in my hands, but I can't describe it. How can you have gold flesh, or glass flesh? Flesh doesn't break like that – I could see the splinters of glass on the floor. Is it because I think I'm clumsy? Was it because I thought that it wouldn't be safe in my hands, is that what I thought? Is that why I put it carefully back in exactly the right place, even though there was no one there to know if anything had been moved? Was it because I could hear his voice again, telling where everything in the house had come from and where it lived? This time I could hear him very clearly saying what I'd only imagined him wanting to say before; that he'd always wanted to see it like this, disarranged. I climbed the stairs, still littered with pieces of clothing. One of the set of pictures on the landing wall, the snow scene, had gone. As I got to the landing and stood in front of the curtain covering the hidden doorway I could hear his voice very distinctly again, saying *Oh, you don't want to see all of that*. I lifted the curtain, opened the door, and for the first time I went into the part of the house I had never been allowed to enter – the white world of Gabriel's hidden corridors. I remember my footsteps echoing even though I was walking as quietly and lightly as I could. I was sure no one was there, but still I walked as if I didn't want anyone to hear me coming.

There was a strange smell coming from the end of the corridor (I've always had a terrible fear of leaving something in the flat and coming home and finding it smelling); right and right again and I was in the kitchen, which was where it was coming from. Just as Mr Clive had told me it would be, everything was immaculate, modern, up to the highest standards of modern hygiene – except that the silver taps were dripping, and the slate worktop was unscrubbed and covered in a terrible mess of oily paper, the remains of several hurriedly opened greaseproof paper packages. There was mayonnaise curdling on the blade of the knife that had been used to cut the string; the handle was shiny with butter, or oil. There were several opened tins, which must have had fish of some kind in them – that was the smell; fish. The doors of one of the cupboards were open, and when I crossed the kitchen to take a look, there was a sort of grit under my feet – coffee grounds on the red and white tiles. There was nothing to eat in the cupboard, only three empty, unwashed milk bottles. So nobody had done any shopping in this house for several days, I thought. I tried the next cupboard, and when I opened that one I was nearly sick. Someone had stacked the cupboard with all the dishes from the dinner party, and even with the heating turned off, the stench from the remains of the lobsters we had been served that night was rising. There were pieces of glass stuck in the pieces of white meat, the big pieces you find when you split the claws open, and there was something moving too. Then I heard the sound of a fly, and I had to shut the door and leave the kitchen quite quickly.

The rest of my tour through the house told me more of the same story; I followed the network of white corridors and there was nothing clean or tidy or cared-for in the whole place. It was as if they had dirtied one room and then just moved on to the next. A half-eaten plate of biscuits and half a cup of cold tea, without a saucer, left perched on the arm of a chair. An eight-week-old pile of newspapers with pieces torn from the back page of each one – the weather reports. An unemptied ashtray, and in every room what looked like a lot more than a week's worth of dust. So now I knew why, on the evening of the dinner party, we had been led straight from the hallway to the parlour to the dining-room; the rest of the house was already filthy. Unfit to be seen.

Except for one room, that is. At the top of the house, I found Gabriel's bedroom. And that was spotless. There were no possessions that I could see, no clothes in the wardrobe. I looked under the bed, and there was no suitcase. The bed itself was faultlessly made, the sheet turned down and the pillow undisturbed; I'd expected that. But when I touched the pillow, to see what kind of linen Mr Clive allowed his staff, the pillow too had more than a week of dust on it.

One floor below, I found Mr Clive's bathroom. There were all the soaps and oils and colognes from Jermyn Street, all in their coloured glass bottles, all ready for him, just waiting for the steam and the endless supply of hot water and the clean skin. Next door was his dressing-room, with its shelves of ironed and folded shirts (no Sunday night ironing for him). The grey silk dressing-gown was hanging on the back of the door (the smell was still there). A whole wardrobe of suits. I hunted along the rail and found the one that he had been having made the first time that I saw him, the dark blue, and held it up against me. There I was, in the full-length mirror on the inside of the wardrobe door; if only I could have done his laugh, his way of looking you straight in the eye, I could have been him – just for a moment. The studbox for the sapphires was empty; the hairbrush on his dressing-table still had his hairs in it. I brushed my hair with it for a moment, copying his style. I was careful to put the brush back exactly where it had been. He had three drawers of socks (day and evening) and two whole drawers of underwear. I should have stolen something really, because of course it was all exactly my size. Lawn handkerchiefs, twelve of them, each one with his monogram done with raised thread, in the same design as he had carved over the front door, the three initials intertwined.

In the bottom drawer, under a beautiful pile of woollen scarves in pale yellows and creams, there was a sheaf of papers tied up with a ribbon, and I got them out and undid the ribbon and spread the papers out on the dressing-room floor. Boxers, swimmers and footballers, all cut out of newspapers, all about nineteen or twenty, and all blond. And underneath them, about thirty or forty sheets of heavy, expensive cartridge paper, each one with what looked like a costume study for a musical. Several of the sheets of papers had samples of fabric pinned to them, and some of them even had buttons and pieces of gold or silver braid. The model was the same in each drawing, as if they were all of boys in a chorus line, as if these were all their costume changes, and so at first I thought they were designs from one of Mr Clive's first nights – I even looked to see if I recognised any of the costumes from that first night at the Pavilion, but none of the drawings of the young man wearing the costumes showed him in a mask. And then, at the very bottom, I found a photo-graph, the only one in the whole collection. It was of Gabriel. *Gabriel* was inked across the top left-hand corner, on the back, and under that, in different handwriting, was written *Gabrijels, Riga*. It showed him standing on the corner of a very grand street, more of a boulevard than a street I should say, because it all looked very Continental. Behind him was what looked like a very smart café, and then across the street an opera house or some grand municipal building, with a small park of ornamental flowerbeds (still bare) and a lake. Gabriel was smiling, and the sun was shining, but there was still ice on the lake, and definitely still traces of snow on the lawns of the park. He looked very young in the photo, only seventeen or eighteen at most, and he was staring straight into the camera, with the same eyes and the same white hair that re-appeared in every single one of the drawings. Gabriel. Gabriel. Gabriel. Then I realised. These were the designs for all his different uniforms. I even found the one for the costume which he had been wearing to serve the dinner party – it had one of the silver buttons and a sample of the dark blue wool pinned to it.

There were thirty drawings, at least. I wondered where all those other outfits had ever got to, when they had been worn. And I wondered what Mr Clive had told the assistants in Haber-dashery and Dressmaking he was doing when he had got all those samples of cloth and buttons and braids.

Because whoever had done the drawings for him, I am sure that Mr Clive had supervised the choosing and fitting of the cloth. As I said, we were alike in lots of ways.

Next door to the dressing-room was the room that I had been deliberately saving until last; the room whose left-hand window looked out over Brooke Street, the room that got the best of the sunlight in the early afternoon at that time of year. I didn't go in, just stood in the doorway, and looked at the open window, and looked down at the unmade bed. Just sheets. I suppose you didn't really need a cover, not with that heating. And not with that body next to you.

The sheets they'd lain on and slept on. The sheets they hadn't bothered to change. Around the bed, the walls were that beautiful dark pink colour, and there were the gold glass lampshades again. Yes, that's right, just like my bedroom. Five Sundays it took, each Sunday a different layer of colour. Of course there wasn't any way I could get the same light fittings as he had at Brooke Street, but when I found those gold pleated-silk shades in Household Goods and Services, I knew they'd do the trick. I wasn't sure I'd got the colour of the walls right when I saw it by daylight, but then on that first evening when I drew the curtains and turned the lamps on I could see I had, and I could see why Mr Clive had had it done like that. It really comes alive. The gold light mixes with the pink of the walls and it's perfect for a bedroom. Perfect for skin. The whiter the skin, the more it takes the colour, the colour of the inside of a conch shell. And Gabriel, Gabriel who came from the Baltic, Gabriel's skin was white. Pure white.

Gabriel's skin against those sheets. That was what I was standing there in the doorway and thinking about when I hear a man's voice shouting *Hello, Hello!* somewhere downstairs.

I didn't decide to do it; I just didn't want anyone, any stranger, to see their bed like that. Do you understand that? I just did it: I got their sheets up off the bed just as fast as I could, I bundled them up and started down the top flight of stairs. I knew that I had to avoid whoever it was and get out of the house unseen if I wanted to avoid any questions, so when I got back along the corridors to the door that led out from behind the curtain on the first landing I paused and got myself ready to run straight down to the front door. It was then, when I paused, that I realised I could smell them. I could smell Mr Clive and his Gabriel on the sheets. To anyone else of course they would have been just a dirty pair of sheets – good quality, of course, but just dirty linen nonetheless. To me – well, I think that at that moment I would have fought for those sheets, fought whoever it was, shouted at them. Nobody was going to catch them, nobody was going to catch them at it, nobody was going to spy on them if I could help it, nobody was going to breathe in the smell of them but me. Nobody else had the right to.

I wasn't thinking all of that exactly.

I was feeling it.

I opened the door slowly, and came out from behind the

curtain without making a noise – but it was no good. The man who had shouted was standing at the bottom of the stairs, and of course he spotted me at once. Just like I'd spotted Gabriel in his flight across the landing on that very first evening.

He was short, and fat, and carrying an open notebook and a pencil. I had no idea at all who he was.

He didn't seem at all surprised to see me; he was quite cheerful about the whole thing. "Ah, hello there!" he shouted up at me, grinning. "They told me that all the staff were gone too, but I'm glad to see that someone has seen fit to stay and start the clearing up. Always so much clearing up to do in cases like this isn't there? Got your hands full, I see!"

He was coming puffing up the stairs to greet me with one hand held out, but there was no way that I could shake it without dropping the sheets.

"Collier. Mr William Collier, W. Collier and Sons, Auctioneers, W1."

I took his hand as best I could, and didn't say anything. I made a good criminal, you see; removing the evidence, not answering questions unless asked to. Especially when the questions are being asked by a man holding a pencil and a notepad. I took to it, you might say. I was just doing what came naturally, Officer.

"And you are – ?"

Let's just say that I told him my name was Jackson.

"Well, Mr Jackson, funny old business, isn't it, bankruptcy. Servants one day and auctioneers the next. And a funny old house too if you don't mind me saying so, Mr Jackson. Been with the family long, have you, or just temporary? – still, must get on, got to get the whole of this place inventoried by the middle of next week, I have. Sale notices already posted. Paintings to plugs, linen to lightfittings – so when you've had that armful cleaned if you could return it to the linen cupboard I should be most grateful, Mr Jackson. And if you could keep that front door shut in future. Looks like we've had some trouble here already, breakages and so on, and I shouldn't want to see anything go missing before the inventory was complete, should I?"

Having made his little speech he didn't seem to require any further explanation of the situation from me. I left him to his notebook; he seemed to be listing the vases first. The door to the dining-room was ajar, so I went in there, hoping that he would carry on upstairs, and that way I'd be able to make a run for the front door.

By daylight, it hardly looked like the same room. The candles were all out, the sunlight was pouring in – and I wonder if Jermyn Street would look like that if they ever let the daylight in – I wonder if I would recognise it, without the steam and the sweat. Everything that I had last seen shining and polished was still there, but shattered, spoilt, rotting, torn. Ruined. Blood everywhere, all over the tablecloth and the carpet, sticky patches of blood on the polish of the table, I couldn't work out where so much blood could possibly have come from – I thought it was blood, you see, because of the smell in there – food, bodies, soiled linen, the smell of something awful having happened. Of course when I'd got over the shock and had a proper look I saw that the stains were actually wine, coffee, butter, and that the gleaming wood of the bare table was sticky with oil. Also that it was scarred with a great gouge right across its centre. In the middle of the table were two things that had definitely not been in the dining-room on the night of my birthday; the picture, which I had already noticed was missing from the landing, and, lying open and face down on the picture, a copy of the Cook's timetable and travel guide.

I knew that the man with the notebook was just outside on the landing, and that I ought to get out as quickly as I could, but I also knew that Mr Clive had left those things there deliberately. If he had been just reading the timetable, then surely he would have left it on the arm of a chair somewhere, not in the middle of the dining-room table. He meant me to find them; he had left them there for me, in the middle of the table, in the middle of the room, in the middle of the house. If he had left me a note, he couldn't have made it more obvious.

I added the *Cook's Guide* and the picture to my bundle of sheets, opened the dining-room door, made sure that the auctioneer or whoever he was had his back turned, and made my way down the stairs and out on to Brooke Street as quickly and quietly as I could. I wonder if Mr Clive's grandparents ever thought of how useful all those soundproofed floors and ceilings would be to Mr Clive and I, how good a house it was to be a criminal in? A good house for men who have to do things where you want to keep the noise down.

Lord knows what that Mr Collier wrote down when he discovered the dining-room like that, or how he accounted for the stripped bed. I suppose his list must still be in a box-file somewhere, and if it is then it must be the only surviving record of the whole affair. Every single item described and priced right down to the last tile and tap and wine-glass (Set Incomplete). *Dining Table, seats eight, mahogany, damaged.* I don't suppose the list mentions my picture, because he never saw that hanging on the wall; it was safely away on the top deck of the number twenty-nine by the time he had worked his way back down to the landing. And I wonder if he ever mentioned seeing me to anyone?

I'm sure he was very efficient, with his pencil and his notebook, that Mr Collier, but even if he wrote down every single thing, no one would ever be able to add up his list and imagine what it was like. They could never really have any idea. "The Property of a Gentleman", that's all he could have written down in the end; nothing about the gentleman himself. Nothing about our Mr Clive as he actually was in those final days.

When I left, clutching my souvenirs, that was the very last time I ever went through the door of number eighteen Brooke Street. So you see, I never did have that final conversation with Mr Clive. Which is why I've spent so many years talking to myself I should imagine.

Oh, he did it beautifully, didn't he?

I didn't go to the sale. I didn't want to see a crowd of strangers in those rooms, deciding how much it was all worth. Sightseers at the scene of a crime, people looking for a souvenir. And besides, somebody might have asked me the way to the dining-room, and without thinking I might have told them, and then they would have asked me why I seemed to know my way around the house so well. *Excuse me, Sir, but could I have a word? Would I be right in saying that you seem to have been here before Sir?* And because I didn't go, I didn't buy anything (I already had my souvenirs) and so you see because I didn't buy anything my name doesn't appear anywhere, not even in the records of the sale. And if a Mr Jackson was ever mentioned by the auctioneer – well, that wouldn't have got them very far. And I don't think anybody at the dinner party would have remembered me. In fact I don't think there is any connection.

All the guests at the dinner party would have given the same story; that's what he told them.

Oh yes, Mr Clive did it beautifully. Perfectly.

And I don't think I've written anything here that would ever help you to find them. I've been very careful on that score, as you may have noticed. He lived at Number Eighteen Brooke Street; that's virtually all you know. How could you possibly track him down? If you are clever then you will have noticed that I've told you that he had his suits made on Jermyn Street, at a tailor's opposite the entrance to the London and Provincial Turkish Bath Company (No. seventy-six), and I suppose you would probably find that they have kept his measurements, and one of the older staff might even be able to give you a quite thorough description, neck, shoulders, inside leg and so on. And then you could use that description to look for me – because you're clever, you are, you've remembered that we looked identical. And you've got my date of birth. And if you found me, then I could help the police with their enquiries, couldn't I?

Making allowances of course for the fact that this was thirty odd years ago and my memory can hardly be relied on, not after all those years, surely.

But how would you find me?

Because I have to tell you (and I'm sorry to have to say this) that my name isn't Page. And it isn't Mr Jackson either; those are names from a play I saw in the West End last year. I've lied to you just like I lied to that Mr Collier. Of course I have. This is nineteen-fifty-bloody-six; I read the papers. If you ever got my real name, you might find out about my darling, there might be some way you could discover him too, and if I thought that for even a minute, I'd burn this, I'd feed it page by page into the gas, even if it took me all evening, even if Mrs Welch came banging on the door and asking what the smell was and was I all right. Not that I should worry really. Even if you got hold of this and then got a sample of their handwriting off every single person who works in Banking – but how can you even be sure of that? After all these years I should hope I know enough to be able to get away with claiming I work in any Department I choose. So you'd have to get a sample from every single member of staff in the House. I don't think so, do you?

Oh yes, I've been very careful. And you have got to be careful, "these days", as Mr Clive always said, especially with the names. That young actor who everyone was so shocked to hear about. That playwright. Those two navy boys and that male nurse at the Regent Palace Hotel. That up-and-coming star from Universal. Any of their names; if they found any of their names in your diary then they'd know straight away.

Somebody said to me in the changing room at Jermyn Street the other day when I told them to keep their voice down, *what are you so bloody afraid of?* Well, I'll tell you. Being up in court and them asking me to name names. Asking me to say his name and address out loud. Asking me exactly what I saw. Them asking me to describe what it was like. Seeing him. Asking *did you know him, had you known him long? Could you describe him?* because yes of course I could describe him. Every part of him. His arms were raised, his hair was white, and he hadn't shaved. What else, your Honour? Anything else?

Had you known him long? I might have your Honour if we had had the time but

I'm sorry your Honour. Breaking down like that.

And the thing is, your Honour, if I can't say it without breaking down, if I just can't bring myself to say it out loud, and so I don't, if you don't hear it from me, then you'll never know, will you? Because those pink walls of Mr Clive's bedroom, you never actually saw them, did you? And let's face it, unless you've got me to do the whole guided tour all over again, those walls aren't pink, and those steps aren't red, not in this December light, and the roof isn't red either and the window isn't open and there is no man standing naked in the sunlight (and his hair isn't blond, it's white), and it isn't two o'clock on the afternoon of March the fourteenth any more. I'm sorry, your Honour, I really am.

Well I think that's almost everything.

Funny how much time there is to think when you take the day off.

I often sit here and look at the picture like this.

I can't imagine my living-room without it, not after thirty-one years, but I can see that it's not necessarily what you would expect in a room like this. It is a bit out of the ordinary, and I suppose I'm not. Very old-fashioned now it looks, "Victorian" I suppose you would say it was. If somebody were to ask, I expect I would say that I had found it in a shop or something. "I don't know why, but I like it", I'd say, and they wouldn't think anything more of it. They'd have no idea.

There were at least a dozen black and white photographs of paintings hanging on the landing at Brooke Street, so the first thing I had to work out when I got it home was why he had chosen this particular one. I put it straight up on the wall so that I could sit here at my table and study it. First I looked to see if there was a label on the back, but there wasn't.

Because of the snow and because of the way it looks exactly like something you would have on a Christmas card I knew it must be a Christmas scene. But then when you first look at it you don't notice the main characters in the story at all. Only after I had counted all the figures in it (there are one hundred and eighty-two people in the picture) did I find Mary, on the donkey, and Joseph, leading her. When I found them I decided that the picture must be of "The Flight Into Egypt", and then I thought I had got the message, and I didn't really study it for a while after that. It was his way of saying *goodbye, we've got safely away* – just the way that Mary and Joseph escaped from danger, the way that they got safely through the crowd without anybody stopping them. And what I know happens next in the Bible story, the fact that they do indeed get safely right away to a new life in a foreign country, that was what I wanted to believe had happened.

But then I noticed that there are some things wrong with the picture. There are some people killing a pig, down at the front, for instance; well, you wouldn't kill the pig after Christmas, would you; you'd kill it just before, for the Christmas dinner. So I went and looked up the painting in the Orange Street Reference Library on the way to Jermyn Street on one of my Saturday afternoons, and there it was, and there was the correct title: *The Arrival at Bethlehem.*

If you look at it this way, the message is different. It isn't a picture of them setting off for a foreign country, not really knowing where they're headed; it's the opposite. This is a picture of two people arriving somewhere safely. Mr Clive must have dreamt of that each time they changed trains. And it isn't the end of the story. It's just the start of it. Christmas is coming, the New Year is coming, all the new years, even nineteen-fifty-bloody-six, in the end. That's what Mr Clive wanted to tell me, only he didn't have time to write it down, or couldn't find a way of saying it. Or didn't want to leave a note with my name on it; that would have been dangerous.

The proper title makes sense of the crowd which is gathering in the bottom left-hand corner, and especially of the man in the middle of the crowd, the one who is writing a list. You remember, "And it came to pass in those days that a decree went out, etc., that every man be registered." He's the auctioneer at the bankruptcy sale, you see, with his inventory, and the point is that he has no idea of what's really happened, and if you look at the picture that way then Mr Clive is telling me *it's all right, nobody knows but you, Mr Page.* I mean, you would think, a pregnant woman in a blue cloak, riding on a donkey, an old man carrying a bag of carpenter's tools, trudging around Bethlehem late on Christmas Eve and saying *Excuse me, is there any room in the inn?* well, you'd think someone in the picture would notice, wouldn't you? But no, they are too busy making their list. And that's just what happened: two men all alone in that house, eight men around a dining-table, a naked body in the middle of the afternoon, you'd think people would notice, wouldn't you, but they don't. Mr Clive and his painter were right about that.

Above Bethlehem the sun is going down, and it's just like the sun going down over Oxford Street with the cold weather coming on when I left work on the twenty-third; one hundred and eighty-two people hurrying to get home, and every one of them too busy to notice what is actually happening. And there, in the middle of the crowd, is me. You wouldn't notice me unless you were really searching, really trying to work the picture out. But there is one person out of all those one hundred and eighty-two people who is staring straight at you – yes you. Can you see him? Keep looking.

It's the ox. There has to be an ox, doesn't there, along with a donkey, so that they can be standing there together behind the manger when the Three Kings arrive with the presents and everything's turned out all right in the end. I think it's quite appropriate really, that I should be an ox. In attendance. Good attendance figures over all these years. Hardworking, reliable and quite a big strong body, that's me. Works for years. The dumb ox – because an ox can never talk. Can't be done. He can't tell you the story, even though he knows it. The dumb ox, with his great sad eye that you don't notice until you've really studied the painting. And that's me. Me, walking steadily towards the stop for the number twenty-nine and hoping to make it inside before the snow comes again, and I'm looking right at you with my great sad eye. Yes that's right dear, it is you that I'm looking at. You know too, don't you? You know; but it's all right, I'm not saying anything. I couldn't. And I don't need to, do I? – just a raised eyebrow, just a quick look over the shoulder when you're walking off down towards the Haymarket, that's quite sufficient to let you know I've spotted a fellow dumb creature. I can see you. You're one of the ones who knows what this picture means, aren't you? Who knows what is really going on in this Christmas story.

Just the timetable to explain now and then I think I really am done.

When I got it home I went through it page by page, and I have even done that again this afternoon, but that only confirmed what I knew already; there are no markings or underlinings in it at all. No hotel name ringed in pencil so that I could write to him, which I would have liked, to have been able to have written to him and said, yes, I got your message. But there was nothing like that, not even a page corner turned down, so I have no way of knowing what time or even what day of that week they left. If you had seen the house in the state it was in that Sunday then you might have said that it looked as if they'd fled on the spur of the moment – all that clothing thrown around, they must have literally run for it. But now I've gone through the whole story in my mind right to the end, I don't think that there was any panic. I think Mr Clive knew exactly what he was doing. I think he had already ordered the tickets. Isn't it obvious? They probably left on the very same Monday morning that I was telling myself to go back to the rest of my life, my weekday life, Monday to Friday. That's why he wanted me to call round early, before work; he already knew what time they were leaving.

Look I don't want to tell you your job Officer, Officer Maguire, but if you want to know exactly what occurred prior to and in consequence of the incident on the afternoon of March the fourteenth and how people felt and how they carried on, then well you will just have to apply your powers of deduction, Officer. Forgive me for pointing out the obvious, but let's start with the drawings. Every single one was of a young man who looked like Gabriel. But that doesn't mean they were done after Gabriel arrived. Not at all; I think the drawings were there, tied up in ribbon, at the back of the bottom drawer, quite some time before the photograph of Gabriel aged eighteen arrived in the post. I think Mr Clive had already spent long nights looking at those drawings, knowing that one day soon he would be twenty-one. Sitting there with the radio on or the Tchaikovsky music, putting that face and that body he was dreaming of into one hundred and one costumes, wondering where he could find him. Telling himself that the more he thought about it the less he could see any reason why he shouldn't find him. His grandmother had taught him that every single object in the house had been chosen, ordered and paid for, hadn't she? That she had planned every single stone of that house before she even saw it?

Well now of course I was brought up to believe that you can't get what you really want in life by just shopping for it; I mean we tell the customers all the time that we can get them anything they could possibly want, anything at all – that's the whole point of a Department Store, after all – but the one thing that really matters, you can't buy that. The thing you think about when you're on your own in the dark. The thing you wait and wait and wait for. But that is just exactly what Mr Clive did. Went shopping for it. That's what he was doing on Jermyn Street; he wasn't just looking for a suit that would fit him perfectly, he was looking for someone to wear those uniforms in the drawings. That was why he asked me what time was a good time to go, so that he could slip in and see for himself – but carefully, unobserved. That was why he wanted to talk to me, that first time; to find out how somebody else was dealing with the problem, the same situation. Somebody who was just like him in every respect; someone who not only looked like him and was the same age but whose body did and wanted the same things as his body. Someone else who was waiting.

But at some point between that first meeting and Christmas Eve he found exactly what he was looking for. Because somebody out there knew what he was looking for, and sent him that photograph. And then all Mr Clive had to do was to send Gabriel a ticket, and the promise of a salary, and when he got the letter Gabriel combed his hair and packed his suitcase and he set out on his journey across the ice, his journey to that famous and still-remembered White Christmas of 1923.

The only thing that I don't know is if Gabriel knew what he was being paid for.

I don't see why not. I think when he had his photograph taken outside the Opera House – well I should say from the way he was looking at the camera that he knew exactly why that photo-graph was being taken.

And let's be quite frank with each other now, Officer; frankly I don't think Gabriel ever made it up to that bedroom on the servant's floor, not even on his very first night. Otherwise it doesn't make sense.

Otherwise why would Mr Clive have started to empty the house of all the other servants straight away? Otherwise why was Gabriel on the landing, why was he wandering around the family rooms when Mr Clive made a point of telling me that he was in the kitchen? My version of events, with them kissing for the first time on the evening of the thirteenth, well that was romantic, I enjoyed writing all that down and that was why I did it, but actually they were together every night right from the start. That was why Mr Clive was late for that opening night at the Pavilion; because they were already together. That was why he always seemed so tired, so haggard, so strange. That was why he could never take me back to the house, because Gabriel was there waiting for him, sitting naked in the light of the golden lilies with the curtains drawn. Every room in the house hot, empty and silent. Just waiting for them to ruin it. That was why he cancelled his Christmas Eve party at such short notice – the only reason why I slipped through the net was that I was the only guest whose telephone number he didn't have. And that story about losing the staff because he wasn't able to pay them was just that, a story. I think he was saving money, not spending it – after all, what did we ever see as evidence of all that spending, all that waste of money that was supposed to have bankrupted the house on Brooke Street – one stalls ticket for a Cochran revue and half a lobster; nothing. And so when Mr Clive shouted at me across Grosvenor Square, it wasn't because he was going mad trying to work out a way of having Gabriel, it was because he was going mad trying to work out a way to keep him. To keep the only thing that mattered any more.

The birthday party was his cleverest trick. That way, he made us all believe the bankruptcy story, made sure that his alibi was in place and already doing the rounds of the London gossip even before he left the country. And of course by inviting those six men in particular he made sure that none of us would ever say a word about what was really happening between the two of them. He knew exactly what he was doing. He knew all about silence. And when I caught them at it, when I turned up on the doorstep the next afternoon, it was too late for any damage to be done; he could afford to laugh at me, because he had already booked the tickets for their journey. In fact, he probably even had them in his pocket that time he ran into me on the pavement after work. That was why there was no food left in the house, you see, not even any fresh milk; they had bought just enough for the dinner party, but after that they knew they were leaving the house behind. He'd even been reading the weather reports, planning what clothes they would need.

Of course the missing part, the part you probably will have missed, is the reason why he did all this. Why he went to such lengths.

Well he told us himself. It wasn't because he *could* do it, because he was rich, but because he had to.

Because of the man who had thrown himself out of the window, that's why. The man at number twenty-two. The man with the faithful valet.

Because he knew what he was up against. He knew how that man felt. Because he knew what can happen these days. He knew about the dead bodies all over London. The blood everywhere. At the time, it's true, I couldn't see it. I couldn't see why he had gone to all that trouble, but now I do see it. Now I can see the white hair, and the sunlight catching it, and now I know why someone would go to all that trouble. That's how far some people have to go in a city like this one. That's how far you have to go to protect him when he is naked like that with the light coming down over him and his face lifted to catch the sun.

If I had gone to Brooke Street early on that Monday morning, as he asked me to, then I would have seen them dressed and ready to leave, and then perhaps I would have understood. I would have seen them off, seen them walking away down Brooke Street at eight o'clock on a weekday morning, seen them making their escape, and seen just how beautifully he'd done it.

Now, thirty years later, I think I'll follow them.

Just to make sure they got off safely, as Miss Elton Haberdashery would say.

Down Brooke Street.

Across Berkeley Square.

Down under the trees along Lansdowne Passage (that's all gone now, Lansdowne House too). Past the Pavilion, past the end of Jermyn Street. They have a train to catch, but I think they're wise not to have taken a cab – that way there will be no cab driver who could say, oh yes, Officer, I remember, I remember those two gentlemen. Catching the boat train I assumed they were, that would make it about eight-fifteen, Officer, I suppose.

No luggage, just that one briefcase.

You can get a lot of money and jewellery in one briefcase – or maybe he has already sent it all ahead, has had it all wired into some foreign account. Anyway, by the time the solicitors realise, it will be too late.

They're at the entrance to the station now. As they make their way through the rush hour they are like swimmers breasting waves, because of course everyone except them is coming out of the station, heads down; everyone except them is arriving, not leaving. Surely I cannot be the only one to have noticed this extraordinary couple – because this is 1956, isn't it, a dismal Monday morning right at the end of a dismal winter, Victoria is as cold and as grey as it ever gets, we can't wait to get down into the tube or on to a bus just for a bit of warmth – and yet there they are, would you just look at that, dressed for spring on the Continent, and wearing the high Jermyn Street fashions of 1924. Yellow gloves! – no one wears yellow gloves any more – and that pure white hair – couldn't he have covered it? Someone is bound to notice it, to remember which platform they were heading for. They are such a handsome pair – funny, Mr Clive really does look handsome this morning, shaved and brushed and striding through the crowd – well they do say that being in love – and so beautifully dressed. They look neither to the left nor to the right; the crowd seems to be parting before them. Not one head turns out of the whole crowd of one hundred and eighty-two, but then I notice one man who's spotted them (it's the auctioneer, W. Collier and Sons, what the hell is he doing here, and what has he got his notebook and pencil poised for – checking things off on his list I shouldn't wonder); I don't hesitate, I go right up to him before he has time to say anything that might draw attention to them, and Oh no sir, I say, please don't raise your voice and draw attention to them, you see, they're foreign. Both foreign, actually, not English at all, either of them, that doubtless explains their clothes and the way they are walking, the way that Mr Clive is holding Gabriel by the arm which I see you have noticed Sir. So not to worry, and isn't it time you made your way to work?

And now there's someone else who has spotted them (just as well I'm here to deal with all of this), a woman, but she's the sort of customer I'm well used to dealing with, Ah Madam, I say, those were the days, just look at the quality of those gloves, they are the last of a dying breed those two. Marvellous really, isn't it, to see them out by daylight? Don't say anything, Madam; they would think it ill-bred to have made themselves a topic of popular conversation. A Gentleman and his Gentleman – I'm sure *you* understand, Madam, and look at them now, unable to afford a taxi, the Daimler gone in the crash of twenty-six which I suppose you barely remember, Madam, being so young yourself, and a chauffeur of course quite out of the question what with the staff shortages since the war. You can see that they're hardly used to this public transport from their apparent difficulty with the crowd, but I suppose it is something we must all get used to these days. No but don't stare, please, Madam; they have obviously risen early so as to make their departure as private a matter as possible; they have no wish to be exposed to comment. Really, they had no idea that so many people travelled by train! See how the faithful valet guides and supports his master in their time of trial, hoping vainly for an empty compartment – alas, no longer first class, and no longer reserved – ah, how long ago the days of truly first-class travel seem!

Quite, Madam, quite like something from a film.

Oh god, they are holding hands. Holding hands. Someone's going to see, someone's got to see that. You can't do that – ah, no, no, that's it, one of them is blind, that's it, that's what I'll tell people, I mean just look, it's obvious from the way they are walking. That's why they are holding hands as they walk towards the ticket barrier. Steering him through the rush hour like that, it's wonderful really, he must really trust him. How brave even to put one foot in front of the other in a crowd like that.

I know it must be hard, but I wish they'd hurry now, blind or not. And couldn't he let go of his hand now that they are approaching the barrier? They really are getting away with murder. Don't they ever go to the pictures? Don't they know that in these railway station scenes the police always wait until the very last minute and make their move right at the ticket barrier? – but no, look, they've made it past the barrier, their papers all seem to be in order, get on the train now please, please get on the train, only two minutes to go, no, only one minute to nine by the station clock, they are walking away from me down the length of the platform, after all they have been through, these are the last few steps. If they can just stay calm for these last few moments and not break into a run. I couldn't quite see, but as they went past the ticket collector I thought I saw Mr Clive's lips moving. Is that my voice or his on the soundtrack, under the whistles and the shouting, the voice quietly repeating, go on, go on, go on – What? Oh nothing, Officer. Nothing. No Officer. What, me? No, no, I haven't seen them. Of course I haven't – I didn't. I didn't; you really can't be paying attention Officer; I didn't actually see this – I'm only working this out from the timetable, really I can't be sure that they took the nine o'clock train at all.

And after all, Officer, the weather that year, don't you remember, the cold seemed to go on for ever, who can have been sure of the trains anyway? The spring had hardly really begun, and then it turned nasty again, you'd think we'd be used to it in this country wouldn't you but then we always seem to depend on the seasons changing when they should don't we, a bit like always depending on timetables I suppose, it wouldn't do to begin to doubt the weather would it Officer, although personally I think it could even be snow again next week, don't you? Will this winter ever end, Officer, that's what I want to know (Why isn't the train leaving? Is something wrong?)? And fancy them choosing to go abroad at this time of year, in this weather, I'm sure this sunshine isn't to be trusted, I mean, it's all very well wanting to be somewhere warmer, I can certainly understand that, but this would hardly be my time of year to travel from choice. Oh just to think of the distance you have to cover before you get to any of those sunny climes and exotic Continental destinations such as are engraved up there on the portals of Victoria Station – look at them all Officer, please do look up at them, stop scanning the crowd like that Officer, I assure you that I haven't seen them.

The Riviera, the Adriatic, you can go all the way from here you know – yes Officer, I think that *was* the last call for the Paris train, oh Lord, all those whistles blowing and doors slamming, but look, Officer, how can you be sure that you've picked the right train – How can you be sure that you even have the right station? I mean there are so many ways that they could have done it Officer, look, look, I just happen to have a timetable right here, *Cooks Travel Guide for Spring 1924*, here we are. I think this is the page, yes here we are – do you think that might be a clue, Officer? Because perhaps they're not planning on catching this Victoria train at all. Look at all these other trains Officer, here we are, look at this, eight twenty-five a.m. – that's right, they might even have left already, had you thought of that possibility? – 8.25 a.m. to Queensboro', then Flushing, Antwerp – what about Antwerp, that's a definite possibility wouldn't you say? Change at Quai St Michel for Ghent. Or of course there is the Calais train, nine or eleven a.m., connecting with one of the fine, fast (look, Officer, here are all the details) one of the fine, fast steamers of the London, Chatham and Dover Railway Company, which would have taken them on the shortest possible sea passage between England and the Continent, landing them in little more than an hour at the Quay "where trains are in readiness for Brussels and other directions (Vienna, Menton, Genoa and then to Venice or Palermo)". Not that I am suggesting that that is the route they took Officer – as you can see nothing is marked – and if that had been their route then surely they would have needed this as their guide; they wouldn't have left it behind on the dining-room table, would they? Looks to me as if they probably just walked out of the door and got on the first possible train without really having any definite destination in mind, doesn't it, Officer? Paris, probably, I agree. Well, it's traditional in these cases, wouldn't you say? Or maybe . . . look here, Officer; Brussels. Sounds nice. Maybe Brussels. Brussels and the Musée des Beaux Arts, an extensive collection of the works of Bruegel I see it says here, recommended, now isn't that a coincidence. And of course the city does have many other attractions. English Taverns, the main Department Stores on the Rue de la Madeleine, the famous Galeries St Hubert (not unlike our own Jermyn Street I understand), luxury goods for gentlemen in profusion, and look, there's even a map indicating the location of the Turkish Baths, Officer, who would have thought they'd be so considerate as to include that on the map. And after Brussels, well let's see, depart 7.01, then the 23.12 from Cologne, the 9.37 from Berlin arrive Riga at ten in the morning, all on the one train, and it's a sleeper too. Tickets bookable directly at The Travel Agency, Selfridges, Third Floor, I can give you exact directions from here – or of course at Cooks itself, 38 Piccadilly, just around the corner from Brooke Street, couldn't be easier really, he'd have had no trouble organising it all. "Cooks Travelling Coupons offer the modern traveller the hundredfold advantage of having all the difficulties of travel made smooth", well quite. And quite a journey it is too; ice and snow somewhere along the route I shouldn't wonder, spring comes later over there I should imagine. London Victoria, Ostend, Brussels, Cologne, Berlin, Wirballen, Kovno, Riga – did you know that was where the lad was from originally, Officer? – yes, I suppose I should have known that you would be aware of that. Personally I didn't even know where it was on the map when I saw it written there on the back of that photograph.

Funny to think isn't it Officer how that journey was one you could make then and that you can't make now. Even the country has disappeared, I mean how on earth are you ever going to find them now?

No, you're right, Officer. It certainly isn't my place to speculate as to their possible destination or whereabouts at this point in time. I wouldn't dream of it. I am fully aware of the possible consequences of incorrect information. Rumours and cross-examinations and details in the newspapers and anxious nights and the next thing you know somebody is reading a suicide note. Yes, really, suicide, all the time. Didn't you know that Officer? I'm surprised to hear that. People will talk, you see, people will – and here's me talking and talking and stopping you getting on with your job and keeping a proper look out for them Officer. Good lord that really is the whistle going now. All abroad! And here's me talking all the time and distracting you from the proper execution of your duties and you didn't even spot them – oh there they go, safe for ever now, just out of your grasp, there they go, into the winter weather.

Midnight.

And about time too.

I've cleaned, and I've cleared away the remains of that Christmas dinner so-called that's been sitting on the sideboard since Monday.

I have been having a weep while I have been clearing away and getting ready to write this last bit. Just as well I decided to spend the money on a good thick carpet, because I don't mean just crying. I mean a good proper howl. What you can't hear can't worry you, can it, Mrs Welch, down there? And what you don't worry about you can't imagine. Don't expect you'll be imagining me howling like that when we pass on the stairs tomorrow and you say "Good Christmas then?". A grown man half-naked taking three days to summon the nerve to clear away his Christmas dinner and even then having to stop for a bit and hold on to the back of a chair until his knuckles are white, he is weeping so hard. Weeping until the muscles in his chest hurt. Until his chest is wet, look at me. I was always scared, you see, that if I ever started then I wouldn't ever be able to stop. I didn't think I'd be able to find a reason to stop.

I suppose you could say that the last four days have been a sort of practice for what I've got to look forward to now, couldn't you, Mrs Welch. Being a widow yourself. Getting in, locking the door, turning on the gas, opening some tins and thinking, what kind of a dinner is that? Turning on the radio to fill the silence. Making an effort to keep the place tidy even though there isn't anybody to keep it tidy for. Because they always end up on their own, don't they, Mrs Welch? I know you never did like to think of me up here on my own, especially at the weekends. Although you never did say anything. And if I go before you do then you'll be up here talking to the people who do the clearance, there not being any family, and that's what you'll say, how funny to have been neighbours and never having imagined his place would be like this. *Same floor-plan as mine of course, kitchen, bathroom, bedroom, sitting-room, separate toilet, but very different in feeling. Quite plain, manly I suppose you'd call it, and two chairs, one either side of the gas which I thought was rather sad, seeing as how he was so much on his own. Always made the best of himself he did, always very well turned out on the stairs in the mornings. No pictures or ornaments to speak of, except for one rather gloomy piece over the gas, though I rather liked the frame. He did keep the place spotless, I'll say that for him. Lovely bathroom things, lots of soaps and oils and such like, and I must say the bedroom was rather a surprise. That lovely dark pink is most unusual, but very effective. I wonder where he got the idea from? Lovely linen, I couldn't help noticing, family stuff I suppose, those big heavy sheets they used to have. Nothing much to tell you what he was like as a person but then I suppose when somebody is gone all you do see is the emptiness. A lovely carpet. I wonder what is going to happen to that, it seems a waste, Wilton I should have said it was, quite a touch of luxury that was, which explains there never having been any noise, I suppose. I think the worst part of the whole business must be knowing that they are going to end up on their own like that. Funny, isn't it, to have been neighbours all these years and never to have known*

and you never did know, did you, Mrs Welch? About our Saturday afternoons up here with the curtains drawn and the gas on. My darling standing in front of the fire on a towel waiting for me to pour the oil over him. "Who needs Jermyn Street now?", he used to say to me. You can't imagine the trouble I had getting the oil out of those sheets. Our Saturday afternoons, and then the pictures as well if we could be bothered to get out of bed, the Empire Leicester Square. And then those two Christmases we spent here together. Me getting the chair to go opposite mine, since we seemed to be needing it more often. Getting used to cooking for two.

Which is why it has taken me three days to clear away that

dinner, Mrs Welch, because I cooked enough for two. Because I still want him to be here to eat it.

I was beginning to get used to seeing him across the table.

So of course when we had arranged for him to come over here a bit earlier than usual, for lunch, of course I had got the table all laid out ready. My actual birthday had been on the Friday, and we hadn't been able to see each other because of work, which is why he was coming over for lunch on the Saturday, to make it special. Saturday the fourteenth of March. One o'clock he was due, and I'd got it all nice and ready. Nearly an hour I waited before doing anything, and an hour is a long time when you are Mr Punctuality like I am. You can get very worried in an hour.

I blame myself for that now. I've had all the obvious thoughts – if only I had gone round sooner, I should have known, etc., you know the kind of thing.

As it was, it was nearly two before I went round to his place.

Before I went round to where he lived, which was something we had an agreement that I would never do except in an emergency.

The door was locked, and I rang and rang but nobody came. Which shows that I must have been frightened enough not to have been thinking, because there was no need for me to have rung, I could simply have used the key and gone up and surprised him. We had got as far as exchanging keys, we had got to that stage, but we had said that it was only for emergencies – that was the sort of thing that we had to worry about, you see, meeting a neighbour on the stairs and being asked who you were and why you had a key. But there was no one on the stairs. Climbing them took forever, because I was so frightened I suppose. But I wasn't shocked; I think I already knew. I wasn't really surprised when the door of his flat itself was unlocked, when it swung open. I know that I should have run straight into the bedroom, I know that, but I didn't. I blame myself for that too some-times, I tell myself that I could have got to him in time. I could have.

I don't think anybody in London can imagine what it has been like some nights when I have sat here and said that to myself over and over again, I could have got there on time, I could have.

I went to the bedroom doorway and stood there and looked down on the bed.

And now that I can write down the last part of it, here finally is the whole of the dream.

I have walked down Oxford Street, and I turn left. Gilbert Street. Right on to Brooke Street. Past number twenty-two. I cross over on to the dark side. The roof is red, the walls are red, and there are the windows of the servants' rooms, and there are the three full-length windows and the balustrade. And one of the windows is open. The left-hand one. And standing there in the window is a young man, naked, stretching his arms above his head. He hasn't shaved. His hair is white, his eyes are closed, and he doesn't know that anybody is watching him. It is two o'clock, two o'clock on the afternoon of March the fourteenth. I cross Brooke Street, I climb the steps, I ring the bell. The door swings open. And now there are the stairs, there is the turkey stair-carpet, the stair-rods, and here is the curtain, here is the next door, and I make my way down the corridor. I arrive at the bedroom. I arrive at the final door. I stand in the bedroom doorway. And I look down at the bed. And of course this isn't Brooke Street. This isn't the bed in Brooke Street that he's lying on, waiting for me, although just like in Brooke Street he is naked, and he has his arms up over his head. Once again it is the first day of the year that the sun has had any real warmth in it, and the curtains of the bedroom window are open. The light is falling across the bed, and from the way he is lying he looks as if he is trying to lift up his face to the sun. He hasn't shaved. His eyes are closed, and in this light his hair really is white, pure white. My darling was lucky with his hair; mine has only gone grey, but his was pure white at fifty.

I look at his face in the sunlight and I try to say his name, but I know already that even if I could make a sound he wouldn't smile, he wouldn't turn. I know that. Not even if I say "Look, it's all right, get up and dressed, and we'll go; we'll leave, we'll find a place. I've got enough money for the tickets. I'll get them from the Travel Bureau first thing on Monday morning." Not even if I said that. So I look down; I look down at my watch. And I'm not in Brooke Street, the walls aren't red, and the roof isn't red, but his hair is white, and he is naked, and his eyes are closed, and it is two o'clock. Two o'clock on the early afternoon of March the fourteenth. Two o'clock on the early afternoon of March the fourteenth, 1954.

1954. Like I said, thirty years it's taken me to get to the top of those stairs.

Yes, I'm all right now, thank you.

Goodnight. Goodnight darling. Goodnight.

ROCK'S SHAME ON THE DAY
HE MET THE QUEEN

Tragic filmstar Rock Hudson was hiding a guilty secret when he attended a London film première.

Just days earlier the gay actor had been thrown out of an all-male Turkish bath after being caught in a homosexual embrace.

Former masseur Mr John Maguire last week recalled: "There he was, this big handsome filmstar – and it was clear what he and the other man were up to."

Rock was in Britain to film for Universal with Yvonne de Carlo and Maxwell Reed. The 6ft 4ins beefcake star chatted to the Queen and Prince Philip at the 1952 première of Mario Lanza's film *Because You're Mine* in the Empire Cinema, Leicester Square. It is a five minute walk away from Jermyn Street – the scene of the shameful baths encounter which could have wrecked his career.

Speaking for the first time since he ordered the Hollywood idol out Mr Maguire said: "In those days we did have trouble from homosexuals who used the baths. Mr Hudson never took a Turkish bath, just spent hours wandering around naked except for a towel wrapped around himself. At the time I was sure that he came in here to pick up boyfriends. I couldn't believe it at first. The day I caught him I was surprised, because his friend was a lot older. I didn't think twice before throwing them out.

"It's funny, isn't it. For years I have known the truth about this fellow and now the whole world knows."

Daily Mirror, London, April 10 1985, quoted in *The Lost Years*, Martin Peck, ed., Cassell, London 1995

Friday, Twenty-Ninth of December

Ten o'clock (morning). At work.

I told them my story about a bad cold and needing a day off and they believed me. In fact, all the questions about Christmas, I could answer them all.

The snow had almost all gone this morning, you could see the earth again from the top of the twenty-nine when it passed the yards at Euston. They say that the snow is like a blanket, and it is true that when it goes and you can see the bare earth again it is like a blanket being pulled off you. And then all the pipes start leaking and things start coming back to life, because you think that the earth is bare, but it isn't, it's all lying buried there ready for the thaw. All those stories about bodies coming up out of the ice in the spring are true I think.

Lunchtime.

Today is the second day at work. All of Thursday and now Friday morning as well I've got through. Having this here helps. I surprise myself sometimes – actually bringing it in to work, even if I am only doing the actual writing when I'm locked in here in the toilet. It's not something I ever would have done before – well, before I started all this. They said to me, "Not having lunch then?" and I said, "Oh no, you know how it is, I think I ate enough over Christmas to last me the week," and they laughed and believed me and left me alone. Starving, actually.

Funny thing this morning. They called the whole Department together just before opening and told us that on Sunday some company is going to use us as a location for a film, a thriller I think it is, and some of us are needed as extras. They read out a list and yours truly was on it. I shan't mind at all, in fact, I quite like the idea. I have met a film star before, after all.

They explained some of the story – not the whole story, that's the thing with making a film apparently, it's better if you just know the scene that you're in, not the whole story and how it ends. That way you can act naturally. Also they told us that it is very important that none of us looks at the camera or pays any attention to the main characters, we've all just got to carry on as normal, because as far as we're concerned, of course, nothing dramatic is happening. Anyway, in this scene there's going to be someone who has to get away from the police, and he comes out of the lifts and cuts through the Department. I didn't say anything, of course, but what I wanted to say was well if this person is trying to get away with something he ought to stop and ask me, really, I'm the expert. I could certainly give him a few tips on how to get away with things.

I wonder if we might see him at Jermyn Street on Saturday; if we do, then I think I might say something. I'm sure those Hollywood boys all tell each other the best places to go, and it won't be the first time (naming no names) that we've had a young man from the Universal Studios (that's the company) paying us a visit. I'll tell him to watch out for that Mr Maguire, that's for sure.

One of the girls asked what the title of the film was going to be, and that didn't half make me smile, because they're going to call it *Nowhere To Go*. That was the first thing I ever said to my darling, you see. Second Saturday in July, 1952, that was. Just a usual Saturday, except that this film star was in. Upsetting everybody of course, though we were all pretending not to look. He wasn't quite as famous then as he is now, but he was twenty-three, and he was six foot four or three at the very least, and, well, you don't get bodies like that in the London and Provincial very often. But there he was, suntan and everything, bold as brass. Lovely.

There is always a very special moment in the steam room on a Saturday when the steam finally does the trick and you relax and let yourself go. You let your head go back and your eyes close and you can finally feel that you've got the rest of the week, all the Monday to Friday, coming out through your pores. The steam gets right to work and you can feel all the muscles unknotting one by one. I count them as they go; quadriceps, triceps. Your fingers are usually the last to go, but if you let them go too you can feel them just hanging there, and you know they've forgotten all their usual weekday jobs too. All that buttoning and lacing and knotting, collar and shoes and tie. They couldn't button you up even if you asked them to.

And then when I opened my eyes, there he was. This great big gorgeous young man, with his black hair dripping. His arms were really wonderful, even better than in the photos they did in *Films and Filming*. Really like marble arms come to life. There was one bead of sweat that I watched tracing the muscles on the top of his arm, running down very slowly – everything was happening very slowly – running all the way down from his tricep to his wrist. Lovely, really lovely. That was all that was happening – me looking at his lovely left arm, no touching, no towels undone, nothing like that. And all he did was open his eyes and look at me and I looked at him, and he smiled, and I smiled. Those wonderful teeth that only Americans have – and then that of course was when our Mr Maguire came in.

"All right, you two, out. And you, son, you want to be a bit more careful, in your situation."

Well of course there's nothing you can do when he says that, there's nothing you can say; there was no point in a scene and no one ever makes one because you just have to leave it for a few weeks and then he lets you back in anyway, he knows what the score is. But I was angry, really angry, so angry I must have been changed and out on to Jermyn Street in less than five minutes. When I got outside he'd gone, I could just see him walking off down towards the Haymarket. And then this voice next to me said, "Excuse me, will I do instead?"

And it was my darling.

I hadn't even seen him; he told me later he'd been looking at me all afternoon but I'd been too busy waiting for our movie star to get into the steam room to notice, and that he'd hurried and got changed and followed me out as soon as he saw I was going, but by then I was too busy being in a huff to notice. *You nearly missed your chance*, was what he said to me later.

He looked me up and down, and I said, "Sorry, nowhere to go," which was what I always said, just as a matter of course.

And that could have been it, I suppose; I really could have missed it.

But just then a taxi came down Jermyn Street from the St James's end, and without even thinking about it I did something I had never done before, something that would have made Mr Clive really laugh I think, something I would never normally do, not me, not Mr Page, not Mr Page, Banking, who had just spent thirty years taking the number twenty-nine; I hailed the taxi. And when it drew up, I didn't say anything, I just opened the door.

A bird in the hand is worth two movie stars in the bush, or something like that.

And my darling smiled, my darling got in the taxi, and my darling came home with me.

I didn't care, you see. I suddenly and for the very first time in my life didn't care about giving the driver my address and I didn't care if anyone was watching me and I didn't care if Mrs Welch saw me arriving in a taxi with another man. I just wasn't myself, that's all I can say really. Funny how that could happen after all those years.

And I wasn't myself all that first afternoon; when we got in we couldn't get our clothes off quick enough, and he was in such a hurry, he tried to pull my shirt off without unbuttoning the cuffs, and tore it. And I didn't stop him; I helped him. And when he kissed me, he hurt me. When it's like that, when things like that happen, it's not just about liking the look of someone, is it? No one was more surprised than me. Two old boys together, that's not what anyone expects, especially not the old boys concerned. Whenever you're in the changing room and someone says *oh look at that*, it's never one of the older men, it's always someone young who's just walked in. And that's how it's supposed to be, according to most people, us old boys looking at the young ones but never touching anything, certainly not touching each other. Look but don't touch. Keep on saying to yourself, that's not for me, it won't ever be me. Well that's just the thirty years speaking. Because it didn't feel like two old boys at all that afternoon. It felt like 1924. It felt like Mr Clive must have felt when he saw his darling with the white hair for the first time. It felt like I just couldn't wait any longer and that I didn't have to either. I was seizing my chance, when I hailed that taxi. I was deciding what to do in my situation. Not deliberately, and not as cleverly as Mr Clive did it, but doing it none the less. Mr Clive stole his Gabriel away, took him where no one could touch him, and I stole my darling away too.

In the snow scene on the wall at home there is a father looking down at his boy playing on the ice. Letting him play but never letting him out of his sight, never letting him get too far away, so that if he hears the warning crack of the ice he can grab him quickly. Now I know that with my darling I didn't hear the warning (no one heard it), but I do know how that father feels. I used to look at my darling lying asleep just the way you see dads looking at their children sometimes. How they look at them when they are sleeping and they try to imagine the years ahead. People do die; people do die in bad winters. You hear these stories and they're true. I always knew that, although I never thought it would happen to me. When a woman is pregnant and the baby dies they say that she carries it right up under her heart. That is where my darling is now. Right up here under my heart.

If ever Mr Clive returns, that is what I will talk to him about; that is what we will have to talk about when we finally get to continue our conversation after all these years (because I know I will never be able to talk to anyone else about it. I may surprise myself sometimes but I could never go that far). He'll send me a card out of the blue to say that he's coming, he'll tell me what time train they're going to be on – and then there he'll be, after all these years, as calm as you like, still wearing the dark blue cashmere coat, walking towards me and laughing and asking me how I've been. They'll both be older, of course, and I will be too, but Mr Clive and I will still look just like each other, and Gabriel will still have his white hair. And when they have found a hotel and unpacked and we've had some tea and it's time to sit down and really talk he'll ask me how I've been and I'll tell him, I'll tell him all about my darling. I will tell him that of course some nights when I get home and turn the key it does break over me like a sweat that he will never ever be there again, but that I am managing, thank you. I'll tell Mr Clive all about him, his hair and his face and his arms and our afternoons, all about our two years together, and then when we've talked about all of that we'll talk about the thirty years as well. And he can tell me if I managed to work the story out right, if I was right about the staff and the timetable and the wrecked dining-room table and the picture.

And then of course I'll have to tell him that the house isn't there any more, that there are no red roof tiles and no red stone walls on Brooke Street any more, no number eighteen in metalwork over the golden glass pane set into the front door, no steps or stairs to climb. But I'll try and tell him that for me as well as for him there is still a naked man with white hair in the sunshine. Because never forgetting, never forgetting a single detail, that is what matters. After Christmas comes the new year, and it's a bit early for New Year's Resolutions I know but here's to a new year for both of us, Mr Clive, wherever you are. And whatever day it is, it can't be very long now until March the fourteenth, it can't be very long until two o'clock on the afternoon of the fourteenth of March comes round again, it can't be very long to wait. It can't be.

back to the afternoon now. I hate the sales usually but this year I don't seem to mind so much being in the middle of a crowd.

Monday

New Year's Eve 1956

Dear Sir or Madam,

    You are doubtless surprised to be reading a personal letter, but I thought it best to tuck a note into the front to let you know that I don't want you to return this to its owner at the above address, as is the usual request. Please feel free to keep it; I have used up most of the pages, as you can see.

    You are probably looking round now and wondering which of your fellow passengers on the number twenty-nine this belongs to – you do usually see the same faces each day on the way to work, after all; perhaps it's someone you recognise. We're mostly regulars, aren't we, and this can't have been lying on the seat for long, or the conductor would have picked it up. I'm more than likely to be still on the bus – unless we've already passed the Dominion. However, I should tell you that it's unlikely that you'll be able to spot me, because there's nothing really about me that is striking or worthy of note. The only thing that might identify me is that some mornings I must admit that I find it difficult to put on a brave face, and so if you are looking round, look for an old boy whose eyes are brimming. Shining. Please don't speak to me, though – not on the bus in front of everyone like this, I shouldn't like it. If you do speak to me, I shall just say, *yes, I am quite all right, thank you. I am quite all right now. Thank you.*

yours, faithfully,

READY TO CATCH HIM SHOULD HE FALL

At three in the morning, to the sound of slow music on the piano, beneath a ceiling shining with artificial stars, in the darkest corner of the best bar in the city, with everybody watching, two lovers fall into each other's arms . . . one is older and wiser; one is just nineteen.

Then follow the rites and ceremonies of a love affair and a happy marriage. From the kisses of courtship to the reading of the banns; from the wedding to the lovemaking to the moment when the first child is cradled in the loving parents' arms, everything in this story is in its proper place. Except that this happy marriage is a marriage between two men, and the bar which is the scene of their courtship is like no bar you've ever been in.

Neil Bartlett's first novel is a celebration of love. It movingly blends past voluptuousness with the stark reality of life for gay men in London today.

WHO WAS THAT MAN?
A Present for Mr Oscar Wilde

'A passionate attempt to fix what is essential in Oscar Wilde, fraud and martyr.' **Adam Mars-Jones**

'Neil Bartlett has grabbed history by the collar and made bitter love to it. I can think of no other way to describe this fantastic personal meditation on Oscar Wilde and the last hundred years of English homosexuality. At the very moment gay existence is endangered by disease and a renewed puritanism, Bartlett has embraced what was alien and criminal or merely clinical and loved it into poignant life.' **Edmund White**

'A valuable counterpart to Ellmann's perhaps excessively balanced biography. Bartlett engages in furious dialogue with Wilde, illuminating modern gay life and that of the 1890s in the process.' **Simon Callow in the *Sunday Times***

'Documentary reports are mixed with personal confession; extraordinary flights of speculation and memory are punctuated with direct questions to the onlooker. In performance, Bartlett is alternately friendly and threatening; in his writing, there is a similar mixture of exhilaration and discomfort.' **Rupert Smith in the *Pink Paper***

'An extraordinary book . . . cruising across the past century, Bartlett analyses faces, words and every scrap of evidence to build up a picture of homosexual London.' ***i-D***

Sitting up reading late at night, the author reflects on the links between the homosexual of the 1980s and his counterparts of a century ago, between gay lives today and those of Oscar Wilde, his friends, lovers and acquaintances. Many books have been written about Oscar Wilde. *Who Was That Man?* is unique – the acting out of a love-hate relationship between Wilde and a gay Londoner of today.

Five-Star fiction from Serpent's Tail

Mr Clive & Mr Page   Neil Bartlett

Gone Fishin'   Walter Mosley

The Silent Cry   Kenzaburo Ōe

Altered State: The Story of Ecstasy Culture and Acid House   Matthew Collin

'Undoubtedly the most exciting development coming in 1998. Puts the bite back into books.' **Ian Brereton, Waterstone's**